THE TRUTH ABOUT Las Mariposas

OFELIA DUMAS LACHTMAN

PIÑATA BOOKS

PIÑATA BOOKS
ARTE PÚBLICO PRESS
HOUSTON, TEXAS

This volume is made possible through grants from the City of Houston through the Houston Arts Alliance and the Exemplar Program, a program of Americans for the Arts in collaboration with the LarsonAllen Public Services Group, funded by the Ford Foundation.

Piñata Books are full of surprises!

Piñata Books
An imprint of
Arte Público Press
University of Houston
452 Cullen Performance Hall
Houston, Texas 77204-2004

Lachtman, Ofelia Dumas
    The Truth about Las Mariposas / by Ofelia Dumas Lachtman.
        p.   cm.
    Summary: When sixteen-year-old Caro Torres goes to help her Tía Matilde at her bed-and-breakfast in Two Sands, California, she ends up also helping her aunt fend off the attempts of her ex-husband to buy the property and steal the treasures that are hidden there.
    ISBN: 978-1-55885-494-9 (alk. paper) [1. Bed and breakfast accomodations—Fiction. 2. Aunts—Fiction. 3. Mexican Americans—Fiction. 4. California—Fiction. 5. Mystery and detective stories.] I. Title.
    PZ7.L13535Tu 2007
    [Fic]—dc22
                                                                      2007019238
                                                                                CIP

The paper used in this publication meets the requirements of the American National Standard for Information Sciences—Permanence of Paper for Printed Library Materials, ANSI Z39.48-1984.

7 8 9 0 1 2 3 4 5 6   10 9 8 7 6 5 4 3 2 1

For Martha with love and thanks

Chapter 1

The bus jolted to a stop and Caro Torres shot up in her seat, fully awake. She had been dozing for the last half hour. The Pacific Ocean was beautiful, especially on a clear August day like this, but she had been staring at it for several hours and, for her, enough had been enough to put her to sleep.

"What's this?" she called to the bus driver over the rows of empty seats. "A rest stop?"

They were parked alongside a line of small wooden buildings that looked like shops, including one with an open doorway that was flanked by two large pots of red geraniums. The fading sign above the door said, "Bradley's Hardware," and beside it a smaller, but freshly painted sign announced that this was also the United States Post Office.

"This is it, young lady," the bus driver replied, standing up and stretching. "Two Sands. I turn inland now. I'll put your bag on the sidewalk." He swung to the ground through the open bus door.

Once the bus was gone, Caro stood on the sidewalk by the post office, her backpack and her friend Ernie's old duffel bag at her feet. A cool ocean breeze played across her face. It smelled salty and clean and she breathed deeply. A tingle of excitement filled her. She had made it. She was here. But the feeling of exhilaration didn't last long. She stared across the three-lane highway. A few more weathered buildings lined the shoulder of the road and behind them a gentle slope led to the sand. To her right, a few blocks away, a long and narrow wooden pier pushed out into the ocean. The pier was empty. The shops, too, showed no sign of life. Caro bit her lip and scanned the buildings again. She noticed that some had "Closed" signs on their doors or windows. She frowned as she thought, I'm a city girl. Crowds of people I can take, but no people at all gives me the creeps.

Back in Los Angeles she had pictured Two Sands as a tiny town, yes, but one with a white church steeple and cottages with flower-bordered picket fences, all clustered near a cove that had a wharf and berths that held bright little sailboats. There was nothing bright about the long wooden pier across the way. She shrugged philosophically. After all, she couldn't very well complain, she had asked to come here. Actually, she had fought to come here.

"I can do it, Mamá," she had said after they had read her aunt's letter. "I'm good with a vacuum cleaner and I have an absolutely good drivers' license. And you, yourself, said I was a good driver. I know Tía Matilde asked for Louisa, but I'm sixteen and a half. Louisa's not that much older and, anyway, she won't go." Caro knew that her sister Louisa had a special reason for not wanting to go. It's name was Ramón. Caro also had a special reason. Hers was seven years old. It had four cylinders and a manual shift and it was called a Honda. Sure, she'd have to give up the rest of the summer, but nothing much was happening in the barrio, anyway. Actually, it was getting pretty boring what with Alicia still gone in Mexico and Papá keeping such a vigilant eye on her—as if she was going to hold up a convenience store or join a gang or something. So, in the six weeks left of summer, by staying with her Tía Matilde and doing "ordinary household chores" while her aunt's usual live-in helper was gone, she would earn enough to buy Ernie's old car. Oh, and then wouldn't it be great to show the girls from Green Street her wheels, her very own wheels. She *had* to persuade her mother.

"I can do it," she repeated. "Really, Mamá."

"It will take a lot of patience, Carolina," her mother said, her forehead furrowed into a frown. "And that's something you have very little of. My sister Matilde is sweet but she's moody and a bit helpless. What I should do is go myself."

"Oh, no, Mamá," Caro cried, her feelings plummeting. There goes my Honda, she thought. I can't let this happen. "Papá needs you."

"So he says," her mother replied. "No, I'm not going. I'm not sure that you should either."

"But, Mamá," Caro said, using the argument she had worked out overnight, "maybe if I get away from all the bad influences you and Papá say are here, maybe that would be a good thing for me." Mamá gave her a skeptical look and a little smile came and went on her face. There had been more talk after that, but Caro had known that it was all over; she had won.

And now, after a bus trip to Santa Barbara and a local bus to Two Sands, here she was a week later in what looked like a deserted movie set. She swung around. Well, not completely deserted.

From somewhere behind her a telephone had rung and was answered. Of course, Caro thought, her tight shoulders loosening, the post office has to be open. For sure they will know where Tía Matilde lives. She picked up her backpack and dragged the duffel bag close to the open doorway.

"Hello," she called into the gloomy interior of a room that was packed tightly with hardware. Gardening tools, ladders, and painting materials were pushed up against the walls and in between there were narrow aisles stocked with smaller items. "Hello," she called again and walked cautiously through the aisles toward a light that shone in a corner against the back wall. "Is anybody there?"

"Back here," a voice called. "I'm just about to close up."

"I'm sure glad you're still here," she said, addressing a small bald man who stood behind an L-shaped counter in the corner. His glasses, perched on top of his shiny dome, glistened in the single light above him. Caro had trouble drawing her eyes away from them. "I just got here," she said, "and I have to find out how to get to . . ." She dug in her pocket for her aunt's address: "700 Loma Vista."

The man had been pulling things off the counter as she spoke, but when she said the address, he stopped and looked at her with new interest. "So you're going up to Matilde's," he said. "You're not going to try to sell her anything, are you?"

"No. I'm . . . I'm . . . well, no."

"That's good. So what do you want her for?"

What Caro wanted to say was, hey, old man, it's none of your business, but she bit her lip and, instead, said, "She's my aunt. I came to see her. Can you tell me how to get there?"

"Well, sure. Do you need stamps or anything?" When she said no, he locked a drawer below the counter and pushed closed the heavy door of a small floor safe, pushing tight a combination lock and twirling it. "All right," he said, "but we'll have to hurry. Wait for me by the front door." He waved her in that general direction.

As soon as she stepped outside, she heard him lock the door behind her and in a moment he appeared around the corner of the small building, struggling into a dark suit coat. "Come on, come on," he said without pausing, "leave your bag there and follow me. Andy will pick it up."

"Hey! Hey!" she called after him. "Where are we going? I just asked you where my aunt lives. And who's Andy?"

"We're going up to Greg's Market. Andy delivers for him and drives people around too. He'll take you to Matilde's. When he gets back from the funeral."

"How will he know I need a ride?"

"Ever heard of a cell phone?"

"Sure," she said. "It's just that for the last few minutes I forgot we were in the twenty-first century. Sorry." His face held a hint of a grin as he threw her a quick look, but he said nothing.

They remained silent then, trudging toward the long wooden pier. In two dusty blocks they were at a level with the entrance to the pier. They turned inland on what a street sign said was Pier Road. Here, too, the street was lined on either side with small wooden stores, but, unlike those on the highway, these shops were not gift or souvenir shops or short-order seafood restaurants. They were the stores found in every neighborhood: a dry cleaner, a barber shop, a beauty salon, a clothing store, and, at the top of the incline, a market. Only the market was open. Open or closed, they all had black mourning ribbons hanging from their doors.

Caro started to ask who had died and then thought better of it. It didn't take a rocket scientist, she told herself, to figure out that it was someone important to Two Sands. Besides, she'd better save her breath if she was going to keep up with the little man from the post office who was striding uphill more easily than she.

Pier Road slanted upward toward Greg's Market, where the shops ended. The road, however, continued curving up one of the low hills that were strung out behind Two Sands. She was extremely glad when the man from the post office pushed open the door to the grocery and they stepped inside. Greg's Market was large and bright. Its shelves and aisles were crowded with groceries, and, except for a girl standing near the checkout counter, it was empty of people.

The girl wore white shorts and a lime-colored tank top on a tanned and perfectly curved body. Her face was heart-shaped, with large blue eyes and a soft full mouth, and was surrounded by a capful of shiny red curls. Looking at her, Caro was uncomfortably aware of her own slim, boyish figure, of her mousy brown hair pulled back into a ponytail and of the crumpled jeans and not-so-clean running shoes she was wearing.

"Well, hi there, Uncle Sam," the girl said in a drawn-out drawl. "What're you doing here?"

"Looking for Andy. Where is he?"

"Gone to the funeral, I suppose." She shrugged prettily. "Why aren't you there?"

"Had to stay open. But I'm heading for the cemetery. This girl needs a lift to Matilde's. Call Andy, will you?"

"When I finish here." The girl shuffled some papers on the counter beside her. "What's she going to Mattie's for?"

Caro spoke up. "Look, Mr. . . . Mr. . . ."

"Samuels."

"Look, Mr. Samuels, if you'll just tell me how to get there, I'll find my way."

"No. You just hang in here till Andy gets back. This is his home base and he'll be—hey, there he is now." He hurried down an aisle to the back of the store and, in a moment, there was the sound of a door slamming. Caro heard him call something and, almost immediately, he was back inside.

He was followed at a slower, more deliberate pace by a dark-haired young man in walking shorts and a white T-shirt. He was not exactly good looking. His nose was a bit long and a bit crooked, but there was something about his eyes and his wide mouth that made his face appealing. "Stop a moment, Sam," he called.

"Can't. Fred's picking me up at the pier and I'm late already." Mr. Samuels was at the front entrance as he finished. He turned only to say, "He's there already," and disappeared.

The girl at the checkout counter smiled at the young man and said, "Thought you were at the funeral. You didn't go dressed like that, did you?"

"I never thought to go." He turned to Caro. "Are you waiting for me?"

"If you're Andy, I'm waiting for you. Mr. Samuels said you'd give me a ride."

"Sure. How far are you going?"

"She's going to Mattie's," the redhead said. "Who knows why."

"Well, that's not too far," Andy said. "Let's go." He walked over and picked up Caro's backpack. The girl at the counter frowned as she watched him. She opened her mouth with a little intake of breath as if to say something and then didn't. At the entrance to the store, Andy turned and said, "See you, Deb," and the girl shrugged.

Caro followed Andy around the side of the building and up into a faded blue S.U.V. that had seen a lot of use. Even so, the interior was clean and well kept. She dug in her jeans pocket for the crumpled paper with her aunt's address and said, "She lives on Loma Vista."

"I know."

"Does everybody know everybody in Two Sands?"

"No, not everybody," he said with a little grin. He swung the car on to Pier Road, turning left toward the hills.

"Oh!" she cried. "My other bag. It's by the post office. Could we pick it up, please?"

"Sure." Andy made a quick U-turn toward the highway where they came to a stop facing the wooden pier. He took a deep breath and let it out slowly. "We'll have a little wait," he said as a line of cars on the highway inched past them. The line was headed by a hearse.

"Oh, oh," she said, "the funeral procession. Who died?"

He stared straight ahead for an instant and then cleared his throat. "My friend, Bradley Poole. He's . . . he's the mayor's son."

Chapter 2

They watched the funeral cars file up the highway in silence. After a moment Andy shrugged, exhaled with a soft, "Whe-ew," sound and, when the last funeral car passed them, turned left. "By the post office?" he asked, and she nodded.

Once they picked up her duffel bag, they drove back to Pier Road. They wound up the hill silently, passing small one- and two-story houses on the lower slopes and, higher up, the tree-shrouded gates that enclosed several large homes.

Caro saw it all but without giving what she saw full attention. Her mind was working on a puzzle. Andy had said, "my friend Bradley Poole." He had also said about the funeral, "I never thought to go." Why? Almost everyone else, it seemed, was there. But even though she told herself that it was Andy's business if he wanted to be different, the question kept hounding her until they reached the summit of the hill. Then it was the house that stood there that captured her attention.

It had two stories and was painted a creamy yellow, with doors and windows trimmed in white. A sign hung above the porch steps. Blue script on a yellow background said, "Las Mariposas." Flowers were everywhere: in window boxes, along the driveway, in pots on the porch steps. And, yes, there were *mariposas*, butterflies, flying above them. A huge ficus tree grew to one side of the house, its gnarled roots spreading out on an open grassy area that extended to the road. To complete the picture, two puffy white clouds floated in the sky above the house.

"My gosh," Caro said, "what a house. Is it for real? It looks as if it just escaped from a greeting card."

"It's for real," Andy said and turned into the driveway.

"This is it?" No way had she expected her aunt's house to be so big, so . . . so . . . well, so beautiful and certainly not to have a name.

As soon as Caro was out of the car, two large cats, one smoky gray, the other ginger, padded toward her, their furry tails raised in greeting. They glanced dismissively and circled the car with inquiring meows. She followed them and found Andy on his haunches, scratching the gray one behind his ears.

"Hi, Cloud," he said and then, "Wait your turn, Pancake," as the ginger cat nudged him. He looked up at Caro. "These are two friends of mine. They're really Angela's cats, but they put up with me. Boys, meet . . . " He looked up at her with a questioning shrug.

"Caro," she said with a grin, "a.k.a. Carolina Torres."

"We're all glad to meet you," he said, rising and extending his hand. "I'm Andy Morales. And I'd better get your stuff up by the door because I have to turn right around." He put her two bags up on the front porch. "Say hello to Miss Matilde for me," he said and backed the car out of the driveway.

Caro remained at the bottom of the porch steps for a moment, a frown growing on her face. The last hour, since the bus had dropped her off, had been troubling. It wasn't the people; they had been kind. Well, maybe not red-headed Deb; she had been sour. Still, there had been something in the air, something she couldn't figure that was kind of electric and made her feel jumpy. She shrugged off her discomfort. Whatever it was, it was really none of her business. Besides, it was certainly okay here, what with flowers and a pair of friendly cats and an aunt who was expecting her.

The porch extended across the front of the house, with a row of four windows on either side of a solid wooden door. Caro pushed aside her duffel bag with her foot and pressed the bell at the side of the door. She heard a buzzing inside the house and, almost immediately in the corner of her eye, she caught the movement of a curtain in a window to her left.

In a moment the door was thrown open and a slim, gray-haired woman in a cotton skirt and a sleeveless shirt stood in the doorway. "I don't know who you are or what you want with me," she said, "and I'm sorry you came all the way up here, but I can't see anyone today. I'm in no condition to . . ." Her voice broke and a tear rolled down the side of her nose. She brushed it away impatiently and with a shake of her head said, "See? I only opened the door because you looked like a nice kid, but go away, please, go away."

Caro's mouth dropped open. She put her hand up to her face and for an instant said nothing. But when the woman started to close the door, she stamped her foot loudly and yelled, "Hey! Just a darned minute! Stop that, will you!"

The woman hesitated, half hidden now behind the door and Caro went on. "I don't know who *you* are either, but I haven't had such a good day myself and enough is enough, you know? I want to talk to Matilde Reyes and if you're not her, tell me where I can find her because I'm not leaving until I do." The woman closed her eyes, leaned her forehead against the edge of the door, and her shoulders began to shake.

Oh, my God, Caro thought, horrified, she's having convulsions. What am I going to do if she collapses? But her horror was short-lived because the woman pulled back the door and turned to her. She was smiling.

"I guess I'm having hysterics," she said. "First I cry, then I laugh. It happened when you stamped your foot. Just like my sister Mercedes. She never outgrew the foot stamping. So you must be Luisa. With all that's happened, I forgot about your coming. I'm sorry. I'm terribly sorry."

Caro folded her arms across her chest. "*Maybe* you're Tía Matilde. I guess you are. But *I'm* not Luisa. My mother called and told you *I* was coming, but if you don't want me, that's cool. I can handle that. I'll take the first bus home tomorrow. Meanwhile, I need a place to sleep and maybe a peanut butter sandwich. I guess you owe me those."

"Oh, my dear, I owe you more than that. Another apology to begin with. You're Carolina, of course. And I'm Matilde Reyes. Please forgive me. I've had so much . . ." She shook her head briskly as if to clear it. "But first the peanut butter sandwich. Come into the kitchen. I think we can do better than that."

Caro hesitated for an instant. Then, she said "I'm starving," and stepped through the door. The first thing that she noticed was the length of the polished wood hall. It extended all the way to the rear of the house where it ended in a large sunny window. The second thing she saw was the cane that suddenly had appeared in her aunt's hand and the difficulty she was having in walking even with its support.

"Can I . . . can I help you?" Caro said hesitantly.

The color drained out of Matilde's face as she turned and nodded. She leaned against the newel post of a staircase that rose on the left side of the hall and said, "As a matter of fact, you can. There's a crutch by the door of my room. Right over there." A tilt of her head indicated a door by the staircase.

The crutch was leaning against the doorjamb of a room that was bathed with light from the front windows and from open French doors. The muted yellows and turquoise of the drapes and bedspread seemed a reflection of a garden beyond the doors. This is the prettiest room I've ever seen, Caro thought, as she handed Matilde the crutch.

They walked slowly toward the end of the hall. Through open doors Caro had glimpses of a pleasant parlor, a dining room with a fresh flower arrangement reflected on the shining surface of its table. Another room seemed to be an office or a small library; she saw the corner of a computer desk and shelves that held books.

The sunny window in the rear wall belonged to a large room that was two-thirds kitchen and one-third laundry room. On the kitchen side a small table with two chairs was placed beside a low wall that divided the room.

Matilde sank into one of the chairs and said, "Carolina, I'm going to ask you to help yourself. I've overreached this morning. That refrigerator's well stocked as is the other one in the laundry room."

Caro thought, two refrigerators, all for one person? At home all we have is one refrigerator with a freezer top and that's enough for five people when *abuelita* comes to stay. Although she said nothing, Matilde seemed to read the question on her face and said, "I'll explain later."

"Okay then," Caro said. "Are you springing for a coke too?"

Matilde smiled. "In the laundry room fridge."

Caro took a long swallow from the icy can of cola before she returned to the table on the other side of the wall.

"Sit, please," Matilde said. "I'd like to—" She stopped abruptly as a door beside the back window flew open and a teenage girl burst into the room, a thick black braid swinging loosely behind her back.

The girl paused by the doorway, breathing loudly. Her dark eyes widened as she stared at the two at the table. "Oh, Miss Matilde," she said, "I thought you'd be lying down."

"Sara," Matilde said, "I'm *so* glad to see you."

"I had to come back," Sara said. "I just had to come back." Then, with a quick glance at Caro she said, "I thought you would need me."

Matilde said softly, "I do need you, Sara. Very much." She pointed to Caro with her hand and said, "This is Carolina Torres, my niece from Los Angeles. She was about to make a sandwich. It would be a big help if you'd show her where everything is because I think I really do need to lie down." She turned to Caro. "Carolina, this is . . ."

"Please call me Caro."

"Yes, of course. Caro, I'm leaving you in good hands. This is Sara Ruiz, my good friend." Tía Matilde rose, reached for the crutch, and limped to the door where she turned. "Thank you both for being here." She took a step or two into the hallway, then turned again. "Caro, the room you can use tonight is just beyond the stairway. It's all ready. Angela left it that way."

"Thanks," Caro said crisply. To Sara, who was already buttering bread on a wooden board, she said, "Who's Angela?" Then, quickly, "Oh, she must be the helper who had to leave. Hey, I can make that," she added, pointing to the sandwich board.

"It's all right. I always help Angela cook. There's ham and cheese or peanut butter, if you like that better. Usually, there's lots more stuff around, for the takeaway lunches and stuff. But when Angela left to take care of her mother and Miss Matilde broke her foot, well, everything got changed. Then Brad died." She brushed away a tear with the back of her hand. "And that father of his made everything worse. He's been absolutely horrible. Oh, help, I'm talking too much."

Yes, you are, Caro thought. I've heard enough. Sure, I knew that Tía Matilde's helper had to leave to be with her old mother for a while and that was sad, but I didn't expect all this. There's enough misery here for a soap's whole season. And what's with takeaway lunches and that huge freezer? Weird.

Sara was talking again. "Here are the pickles," she said. "I'm going outside to feed the cats."

Caro ate her sandwich quickly. She was thinking of making another when the doorbell buzzed on the wall above her. She waited a few minutes and then walked up the hall to Matilde's open door.

"Want me to get that?" she asked. "Sara's outside."

Matilde was lying on a small couch by the front windows. She raised herself on an elbow and said, "Yes, please. I'll be right there."

Caro opened the door to a middle-aged couple both dressed in knee-length walking shorts and white polo shirts. They smiled broadly. "Hullo," the man said. "We're the Browns, Susan and Will Brown."

From behind Caro, Matilde said despairingly, "Oh, my, I was afraid of this. You didn't get my messages."

The man said, "We've been on vacation up north for over two weeks. When we're on a pleasure trip, we don't pick up our voice mail or our e-mail. If we did, it wouldn't be much of a vacation, would it?"

Mrs. Brown said hurriedly, "Of course, we have our cell phones for emergencies." And then, "Oh, dear, mine has been malfunctioning for some time; we're going to replace it when we get home. But, there's always Will's."

Matilde sighed. "It must have been your number that I talked your travel agent into giving me. Well, come in, come into the parlor. It's hot outside. We can at least give you a cold drink."

Moving awkwardly with the help of the crutch, Matilde led them into the room she had called the parlor. The room was sunny and bright, furnished with comfortable chairs and a cushioned couch that faced a brick fireplace. A row of potted plants lined the front windows.

Caro remained by the door, trying to figure out what was happening. She should have paid more attention to the letter that Tía Matilde had sent her mother. She frowned, trying to remember what it had said: " . . . *so while Angela is gone, I'll keep the guests to a minimum.*" Yes, she remembered that, but she had more or less ignored it. " . . . *But I'm having trouble getting anyone from the town to help me and I remembered what a charming, responsible girl Luisa was. . . .*" When her mother had read that to them, she cried, "Mamá, I can be charming too! And I'm responsible!" She had forgotten the rest of the sentence, but now it came back to her as boldly as a newspaper headline: *"I have to keep Las Mariposas paying now more than ever if I want to hang on to my house. . . ."* Now, standing in the doorway, it became clear to Caro that she had taken on more than she had expected. Las Mariposas was a guest house, a business, of course. And what was she doing here?

"What a lovely parlor," Mrs. Brown was saying. "No wonder our agent said Las Mariposas was the best Bed and Breakfast in the area. Will, look at these lamps and this precious Roseville vase." She turned to Matilde. "Do you think you could give us a bite of lunch before you show us our room? All the restaurants on the highway were closed."

"I can't show you your room at all," Matilde said quietly, indicating her crutch. "I haven't been upstairs since my accident. That's why I started leaving you messages that very day."

Mr. Brown pulled out a straight chair from beside the wall. "Here, sit down, Ms. Reyes. You look pale. Are you all right?"

"Pain," Matilde said. "Our feet have too many breakable bones. And they *all* hurt when one is broken." She turned to the woman. "Mrs. Brown, I'm sorry, but you can see it would be impossible."

Susan Brown blushed and bit her lip. "We'll leave right away," she said. "We'll find somewhere to stay tonight, I'm sure."

"Thank you," Matilde said. "I'm really very sorry." She turned to Caro. "Caro, would you . . . would you please bring these good people something cold to drink before they leave?"

Caro nodded and turned toward the kitchen. As she did she saw Sara coming down the staircase. Sara caught up with her, tapped her on the shoulder and whispered, "Tell her the front bedroom is all ready. I pulled open the drapes and the windows. I put clean towels and soap in the bathroom and a little bowl of daisies on the dressing table."

"What are you two whispering about?" Mr. Brown, a twinkle in his eye, was watching them from the doorway.

Sara's face turned red. Caro said, "Nothing really. Would you and your wife like cokes to drink?"

"There's lemonade too," Sara said shyly.

Mr. Brown followed them to the kitchen. "Cokes are fine and . . ." His eyes had found the sandwich makings. " . . . A ham sandwich would be heaven. Do you think that's possible?"

"Oh, yes," Sara said, washing her hands and starting in on the sandwiches. "Miss Matilde is very generous. But we don't usually eat in the parlor. Will this little table be all right for you and your wife?"

"Perfect," he said. "I'll go get Susan."

While the Browns ate, Sara went into the parlor and explained to Matilde about the room. Matilde shook her head in wonderment, smiled at Sara and said, "Sara, Sara, I see you've taken on the job of guardian angel for me and the Browns."

Sara turned a rosy red. "Oh, the room was easy, Miss Matilde. It hardly needed dusting. And all the bathroom needed was soap and towels."

"You're wonderful," Matilde said with a little shrug. "But, no. They'll need breakfast too."

Sara said, "Angela showed me how to make cottage-fried potatoes. Besides, the freezer's full of Angela's muffins and coffee cakes."

Caro, who had been listening silently, looked from her aunt to Sara and said, "I can make a Mexican omelet. You know, with salsa, if you have the stuff around."

Matilde gave her a long, thoughtful look. "I thought you were leaving tomorrow."

So did I, Caro thought, but I have a car to buy. Ernie's holding it for me. And you, Tía Matilde, look as if you really need help. "How long will they be here?" she asked.

"They reserved for two nights, but they'll under-stand . . ." Matilde left the sentence unfinished.

"I'll stay until the Browns leave," Caro said. And then, abruptly, "Or until you don't need me anymore."

Matilde looked from Caro to Sara and back again. "Two guardian angels," she said with a shake of her head. "You can't ask heaven for much more."

Chapter 3

The Browns loved the room. They loved the idea that Sara and Caro would prepare their breakfast.

"And early morning coffee too," Sara told them proudly. "Only not in the parlor this time."

No, the Browns didn't mind that at all; they loved the kitchen too. The Browns loved every inch of the house. And, now, while there was still some of the day left, they had told them, they were off to find that black sand beach they had read about. Two Sands. So that was the reason for the name.

After the Browns left and while Matilde finally found time to lie down, Sara and Caro cleaned up the kitchen and carried in Caro's things from the front porch to the room with the door under the stairway that was to be hers. Then Sara said, with a quick little smile that Caro was starting to recognize, "Want to see the other upstairs bedrooms? They're really pretty."

"Sure," Caro said. So they went up the stairs quietly so as not to disturb Tía Matilde.

The rooms all had names that were painted in script on the doors. The Browns had the Sunrise Room, all creamy yellows and white, with some still life paintings of pears and bright green apples. The other rooms were the Sky Room, all blues and white, with a painting of fleecy white clouds above a lonely pasture; the Meadow Room, in greens with a touch of gold and a huge clay bowl of pampas grass that matched the tans in the bedspreads, and the

Ocean Room, aquamarines and white, with a milk-white chenille bedspread on a high, full bed. Caro felt that Sara was expecting "oohs" and "ahs," but that wasn't her style. Instead she said, "The rooms are really cool. Who did the decorating?"

"Oh. That was Miss Matilde. She's very artistic. You should have seen this house before she fixed it all up."

"So you've been around for a long time?"

"Forever," Sara said with her quick little smile. "Maybe before that. We live in a house on the other side of the windbreak. You know, that row of eucalyptus trees behind the house." They were going down the stairs as they talked. When they reached the bottom, Sara put her finger to her lips as they skirted Matilde's open doorway. "Sh-h. She really needs to rest. It's been a *very* bad day for her. The funeral and all."

"Was she a friend of the boy who died?" Caro asked as they came to the kitchen.

"Oh. You didn't know? I thought because she's your aunt and all." Sara pulled out one of the chairs by the small kitchen table and plopped down on it.

"No," Caro said as she sat across from her, "I didn't know. What?"

"She's Brad's mom. Stepmom, I mean. Until the divorce, I guess. But he called her Mom all the time."

"*His mom?*" Caro needed a moment to absorb that. Finally, she said, "But she didn't go to the funeral."

Sara looked extremely uncomfortable. "I know," she said. "It's because . . . because of what Mr. Poole did. My mother says only the devil would do what he did to Miss Matilde. But she also says that the saints are looking after Miss Matilde and that he will be punished. I think that's true."

Caro waited for more. But when Sara remained silent, staring at the tabletop and shaking her head, she said, "*What?* What did he do?"

Sara let out her breath. "It was bad," she said. "He got some kind of legal paper that said she couldn't go to the funeral at the church or even at the cemetery. So, even though she wanted to, she couldn't go. My mother says that they'd put her in jail if she did."

Caro nodded. She knew about "restraining orders." Pancho Peña's wife down the block at home had had to get one served on Pancho so that he wouldn't come near her or the children and beat them up. But what had her aunt done that would persuade a judge to agree to such a paper?

"But why would Mr. Poole do that?" she asked. "What harm could she do at a church or cemetery?"

Sara shrugged. "He's a mean man. He's made up all sorts of lies about her."

"But what could he say? About the funeral I mean. Did he think she would set fire to the church or slash the tires of the cars going to the cemetery?"

Sara giggled. "Not Miss Matilde. My mother says she's almost an angel. I guess nobody knows what Mr. Poole told the judge or whoever fixed up the paper, but everybody knows what he's been saying all over the town, and he's the mayor, you know, so he could get that paper easy. And I know you're going to ask, so I might as well tell you. He goes around saying that she's to blame for Brad's dying, that she practically killed him."

"Holy Toledo," Caro said. "What kind of a loser is he? How can he say that?"

"It was because . . . because she loaned him her car so he could go over to Oak Valley." Sara let out her breath and went on. "On the way home the car went off a cliff and fell into the ocean, well, onto the rocks in the ocean at the bottom of the cliff. The car got stuck on the rocks. They got Brad out, but he was already dead." Her voice broke but she added, "They're still trying to bring the car up."

"How horrible," Caro said. "So maybe she shouldn't have let him take the car if she wasn't supposed to, what do I know, but an accident's still an accident."

"That's just it. What he's saying." Sara dropped her voice to a whisper. "He's saying it wasn't an accident. He's saying she loaned him the car so he could . . . so he could kill himself."

"Suicide? Holy cheese! He must think she's a monster."

"No, he doesn't," Sara said matter-of-factly, "but he wants other people to believe it."

"Why?" Caro leaned forward; she really wanted to know. "Why the smear campaign? What does your mother say?"

"She won't talk about that, but Andy says that Mr. Poole wants Miss Matilde to leave town. Andy says he hasn't figured out why yet, but he's going to."

"Weird," Caro said and sat back in her chair. Maybe she had made a mistake in agreeing to stay. But if she went home now after the dust she had raised to come here, she would never live it down. Especially with her father. He hadn't wanted her to come to begin with. He'd said she wasn't old enough to handle the responsibility. Well, maybe he was right, but she really wanted that car.

Sara's face was tinged with pink as she said, "It's not weird at all. Andy loves Miss Matilde just like I do. Just like Brad did. And he's going to help her all he can. And so am I."

Oh, no, Caro thought, I've really put my foot in it. "Sorry, Sara," she said quickly. "When I said 'weird' I was thinking of something else. Honest I was. Of course her friends want to help her. That's what friends are for."

The hurt look on Sara's face relaxed and a twinkle returned to her eye as she said, "How about relatives? Do they help too?"

"Well, sure, I guess so. Oh, you're talking about me. Sure, I guess I'd want to help if I knew what was going on. But I don't. Only that Mr. Poole is mean and rotten. Why did she ever marry him?"

Sara bit her lip and shook her head, and it was at that exact moment that Caro knew that a decision had already been made. She wouldn't change her mind; she was going to stay. And she knew herself well enough to know the real reason why. It wasn't because she loved Tía Matilde the way the others did; she hardly knew her. Or even to buy herself a car, although that was important. Part of the reason was anger. A picture of Matilde's face when she had first opened the door to her, a face streaked by grief and pain, flashed into her mind. How dare he? She also had an uncontrollable curiosity. She had to find out what this was all about.

"I guess I don't know why she married him," Sara said. "I was just a little kid then. But, later, when I have more time, I'll tell you what my mother says about that." She stood up abruptly, her long braid bouncing against her back. "I've got to go now. I'll see you real early tomorrow morning."

"That's right. Breakfast. How early?"

"Like six o'clock."

"Ugh. I'll never wake up."

"Yes, you will. Angela left her clock radio. You can set the alarm."

"Thanks," Caro said, screwing up her face, and Sara gave her a grin and a thumbs up sign as she went out the back door.

Caro had just enough time to unpack, take a quick shower, and appreciate Angela's room before her aunt got up from resting. Angela had made space for her things in a large closet and in the chest of drawers, and left a welcoming note pinned onto the pillows on the bed. It was a long room, with a large roll top desk at one end and a perfect TV corner, with two comfortable chairs and a footstool at the other. The outside wall had four long windows that offered a great view of the ocean. She was looking out a window at the glistening expanse of blue water when behind her she heard the sound of her aunt's unwieldy footsteps.

Matilde paused at the open bedroom door. "I didn't plan to desert you for so long. I actually slept."

"You didn't desert me. You just gave me time for a shower."

"Well. But I promised you an explanation."

"It's okay. Sara put me in the picture. About Brad and the funeral, I mean. I'm . . . I'm really sorry about that. And about your not being able to go and . . . and all that."

There was an awkward silence for a moment and then Matilde said, "It's all right. I'll say goodbye to him another time." She cleared her throat. "Let's go in the kitchen. I need a cup of tea or coffee, or something."

"Good," Caro said, glad for something to do. "I know I can boil water. And I'm good at following instructions, so if you want coffee, walk me through it."

They sat, Caro with an icy coke, Matilde with a steaming cup of coffee, while Matilde explained how things were at this point regarding Las Mariposas Bed and Breakfast. "After I broke my foot, I canceled the reservations through July and the first couple of days of August, thinking that by now I would be able to produce an adequate breakfast for the guests, but the events of the last few days . . ." Matilde paused, picked up her cup and sipped it slowly. "But even if, somehow, I came up with a breakfast for eight, there's more to it than that. There's the shopping, for instance."

"I can do that," Caro said firmly.

"Oh, Caro," Matilde said, "that would help, but the only vehicle I have now . . ." She swallowed hard, " . . . the only vehicle I have now is an old pickup with a stick shift."

"I can drive it."

Matilde threw her an appraising glance and said, "Can you really?" When Caro nodded, Matilde said, "Of course, there's the table to be set with flowers and linen runners—"

"I can follow instructions."

"Yes, you can. Thank you. But then someone has to serve the food and eight people are a lot to wait on. Brad had planned to help me."

"If you tell me how," Caro said, "I can do it." Matilde stared at her over her steaming cup and Caro added, "Sara would help."

"Yes, she would. And María, that's her mother, takes care of the bedding and cleaning. Let me think for a bit. There's no one due until Thursday, so we'd have a couple of days to prepare. My thinking is still pretty muddied, but one thing I know: I can't afford to cancel those reservations." Tears welled up in her eyes. "I won't be driven out of my house!"

Caro stood up. "I'll get you some more coffee," she said. And then with a mischievous grin she added. "How do I pour it? Do I pick the cup up first?"

Matilde looked up at her and smiled. "Okay, Caro," she said. "You're on. We're going to do it."

Chapter 4

When Caro awakened the next morning, she groaned then grumbled, "Joey, stop all that noise." She pulled the blankets over her head and turned over. But when the sounds continued, she threw off the blankets ready to jump out of bed and clobber her kid brother. But she found herself in her bed and in her room at her aunt's house in Two Sands. And the alarm on the clock radio was buzzing.

Caro washed and dressed in less than fifteen minutes and was surprised to find that she was not the first in the kitchen. When she opened the kitchen door, she found that both Sara and Matilde were there. Sara, at one end of the island counter, was squeezing orange juice into a glass pitcher and Matilde, at the other end, was prying off the lid of a coffee can with one hand while she supported herself on the counter with the other.

Caro walked up to Matilde and handed her the crutch. "Sit down, please. You showed me how to make coffee, remember?"

"All right," Matilde said with obvious relief. "Since it's only the Browns, use the six-cup coffee pot. There's an outlet behind the marble-topped cabinet in the parlor."

Sara said, "I'm sorry, Miss Matilde, I made a mistake. I told Mr. Brown the early coffee would be in the kitchen."

"That's what we planned," Matilde said. "But I decided that we three needed to practice for Friday when we'll have more guests. Thank heavens, it's only Tuesday."

Before the coffee was through percolating, Mr. and Mrs. Brown came down the stairs, this time dressed in khaki shorts and hiking boots. At Matilde's instruction Caro met them in the hall.

"The coffee's in the parlor after all," she said, placing a small pitcher of cream on the cabinet beside the coffee mugs. "It'll be ready when the light goes on, but I need to warn you. I made the coffee."

"I'll run the risk," Mr. Brown said with a grin. "It smells great." He turned when his wife spoke.

"Will, come look at this." She was standing in the corner by the front windows, looking with great concentration at a small painting hanging on the east wall. "It looks like a Varo, although it's unsigned. Here in this clump of reeds would be the usual place, but no signature there. Look at it. Doesn't it remind you of the Varo we saw in the Goetz Gallery in San Francisco last week?"

"Yeah, you're right. The one of the pots by a crumbling fence. And the huge price."

"That's a close enough description," his wife said with a smile. "Yes, that's the one. So look at this one. Look at the thickness of the paint and especially the deep gray-green of the reeds. That cloudy green is almost a Varo hallmark. The only thing missing in this painting is a human presence. Remember the man on the road beyond the 'crumbling fence'? I've seen a couple of other Varos, one with a face in a faraway window and the other, a child's head peeking around a tree. They're never central to the subject, but they give the painting a sense of proportion. We'll have to ask Ms. Reyes about this one."

"Good morning," Matilde said from the doorway. "You're up bright and early. I hope you slept well."

"We did," Mr. Brown replied as he filled two mugs with coffee. He took a sip from one, smiled at Caro and said, "It's good and it's hot. Cream, Susan?"

His wife shook her head and turned to Matilde. "We were looking at that painting. I wondered if it could be a Varo."

"Susan's the artist," Mr. Brown said quickly. "I'm not that familiar with contemporary painters."

Matilde said, "That's not the work of a professional painter. My grandfather did it." She smiled. "That's a Papacito. You know how old people take up hobbies in their retirement. Well, Papacito spent hours at it. I don't think he was very proud of his work, because once a painting was finished, he would dump it and begin another. At any rate, we never saw them again. I think painting was like therapy to him."

"How was it that you got this one?" Susan Brown asked.

"He died before he finished it. That's why I kept it. I felt as if I was keeping him alive somehow." Matilde leaned against the door frame and said, "Are you planning to hike one of the Robles Hills trails?" When they smiled and nodded she added, "Maybe then you'd like an earlier breakfast . . . and a sandwich or two to take with you?"

"Could you?" the Browns said together.

"Well, Caro?" Matilde asked.

"Sure," Caro said, pleased that she was asked to be a part of the decision. "Sure. Only it won't be an omelet. Just scrambled eggs. And Sara's potatoes, 'cause she's already browned them and they're in the oven. Oh, and salsa on the side."

"I couldn't ask for anything better," Mr. Brown said. "And a couple of those ham sandwiches will make our day."

When the Browns were gone, Sara and Caro carried in the dishes from the parlor and dining room and Matilde, sitting on a stool, stacked them in the dishwasher. Then the two girls went upstairs to clean the Sunrise Room, Sara explaining how to make up the bed and how personal items, if at all possible, were not to be touched. They cleaned the bathroom, then bundled up the sheets and towels and started downstairs.

"Do we do the laundry too?" Caro asked.

"Well, not usually," Sara said and the uncomfortable look returned to her face. "Well . . . Matt's Cleaners on Pier Road used to do the sheets, but a week ago they said they couldn't do them any more."

"That's too bad."

"I know. My mother and I have been doing them. It hasn't been bad because Miss Matilde canceled so many guests. Starting Friday, my mother's going to come and work with us, thank goodness. Anyway, what you asked. Yes, we should do the laundry."

"Yuck!" Caro said.

They found Matilde in the kitchen seated at the small table. "I've been checking on our food supplies, " she said. "And we're in pretty good shape. Your father's going to bring us fruit and eggs from the Sanchez Ranch, Sara, and Andy's picking up the stuff from the dairy. Tomorrow, Caro, we can go down to Greg's for whatever else we'll need. And as far as laundry is concerned, that's my job for today. Dump that stuff in the washer. I can measure detergent and push buttons even if I can't climb stairs. And, by the way, my two efficient angels, we will *not* be changing the beds sheets every day, not unless we're requested to do so."

"Couldn't we stretch it to a week?" Caro asked with a grin.

Matilde smiled back. "That *would* help, wouldn't it?"

Sara said, "I'd better go now. I put the coffee pot away."

"Of course, you should go. And take Caro with you. I hope you have time to show her around the place."

"Hey, I'd like that," Caro said. "But first I'm going to sweep up the junk we spilled on the floor when we made breakfast." She caught Sara's eye and they burst out laughing. "Cut it out, Sara. You know they loved the rubbery eggs and the slimy potatoes."

"They weren't that bad," Sara said, "and the place mats we used were pretty. All right, you sweep and I'll follow you with the mop. Then we'll go."

Before they had finished cleaning up the floor, the phone rang and Matilde hobbled across the kitchen to answer it. "Las Mariposas. Matilde speaking." A pause then, "Hello, Greg." And then a long listening silence with only an occasional "yes" or "no" and a frown deepening on Matilde's forehead. Finally, she said, "No, Greg, I don't understand. Let's just say that I accept that it's out of your control. We don't need to talk any longer. Goodbye."

Sara had stopped her mopping, a look of pain on her face. "Oh," she said, "Oh, no."

"Yes," Matilde said with a long sigh. "*Dios mío,* another one. That's Matt's Cleaners, the plumbers—thank heavens for your father, Sara—the window washers and

now, Greg's Market. The mayor's twisting a lot of arms.
I'm lucky that the utilities are county services."

"Oh," Sara said. "But your groceries."

"We'll go to Oak Valley."

Sara frowned. "But your car . . . you know, it's . . ."

"I'm going to drive her pickup," Caro said. "I like
trucks. And Oak Valley's not that far, is it?"

"It'll have to be today then," Matilde said. "I'll put in a
call to Alfredo at Al's Market and he should have the order
ready in an hour or so. Meanwhile, you two go on. Rest.
Relax. Whatever."

Sara and Caro went out the kitchen door. Shrubs
hugged the rear wall of the house except for the back
stoop and an old-fashioned cellar door near the ground
beside it. A low rail fence that enclosed the backyard was
almost covered by trailing white roses and, in the center, a
large elm tree shaded comfortable chairs and tables.

Sara started toward a gate in the rear. "Come on," she
said. "I'm going to show you my house."

"Not before you tell me," Caro said, dropping into one
of the chairs under the elm. "Why is that rat fink of a
mayor doing all those rotten things to her?"

"Nobody knows. I told you, remember? My mother
says even Miss Matilde doesn't know. He wasn't very nice
about their divorce, and he didn't like that after it Brad
practically lived here, but nobody seems to know why
he's being so mean now. My father says he's crazy,
absolutely *loco*." Sara grimaced. "I get mad and sad and
all mixed up every time I think about it."

Caro jumped up. "Hey, I'm sorry. Let's go. Show me
your house."

They closed the gate behind them and walked toward
the eucalyptus trees on a dirt path that, like an old scar, cut

across a meadow of drying summer grasses. At the line of the trees the trail turned and started downhill. Here the path was hugged on each side by waist-high shrubs with dark green leaves and pink flowers. They continued downhill in the mottled shade of occasional trees. The trail now wound around large rocks and masses of low-growing vines.

"Watch out for the poison ivy," Sara said.

"Where? I'm a city girl, remember?"

"There," Sara said, pointing to a red-leafed vine near the path. "Leave that alone. Come on, we're almost there."

Caro said, "Hold it. I hear water. Is there a river down there?"

"Too little for a river," Sara said, grinning. "It's hardly big enough to be a brook even. It's called Reyes Creek after Miss Matilde's grandfather. Your great grandfather, I guess. I'll show you."

In another few steps they were standing on an opening above a fern-filled bank. Below them the clear water of a narrow creek flowed gently westward over a bed of rounded stones that reminded Caro of a cobblestone path. At the edge of the bank a mass of smoky green reeds pushed up from the water's edge. Directly across from them on the opposite bank stood a narrow wooden structure not more than one foot deep, two feet wide and, perhaps, five feet high. It was like an open cupboard. It had a peaked roof, with a shelf near the top that held a small framed painting and a glass with yellow daisies.

"This is our special shrine for *la virgen de Guadalupe*," Sara said proudly. " We bring flowers and pray here. The guests from Las Mariposas all love it."

"How do you get to it? How do you cross the creek?"

"We don't," Sara said and the twinkle was back in her eye, "not usually. We come down the trail on the other side of the creek. It goes all the way to the town and ends up near Pier Road."

"Cool," Caro said and turned back to the little shrine. "Hey!" she cried. "This is the place in the painting. The painting in the parlor."

"That's right. That's why I showed it to you from this side. The first *virgen* in our shrine was one Don Armando, you know, your great grandfather, painted, but it was stolen. Even though all the way down the hill on both sides belongs to Miss Matilde, once in a while someone sneaks in and steals our *virgen*. When that happens my mother just buys a new one. She says the new one becomes real and holy the minute we pray to it. And will you wait, please," Sara said, dropping to her knees, "I'm going to say a prayer right now for Brad and Miss Matilde."

Caro turned away and took a deep breath. The air was cool and sweet with a tang of the nearby ocean. She closed her eyes, drinking in the restful sounds: the whirring of a bird's wings high in the treetops, the soft scurrying of a small animal in the underbrush, and behind it all, the gurgling trickle of the creek as it wound downhill. When she opened her eyes Sara was standing, and they started back the way they had come.

At the top of the hill, the path divided into two trails. One led through a jumble of trees to a rough wooden bridge that crossed the creek. Sara took the other. It went through the eucalyptus trees to a cleared space in which stood a small house painted white. A rope swing with a wooden seat hung from a branch of a large sycamore tree in the front yard.

"Those are walnut groves behind the house," Sara said. "And down the sides of the hill too. My father used to be in charge of them. You know, when there were pickers and other workers too."

"Wow," Caro said. "Real walnuts. Like right in your backyard."

"There are just a few now. Trouble is the trees are no good anymore. Most of them are dying. When Mr. Poole married Miss Matilde he brought in a lot of expensive experts to make the groves healthy, but nothing worked. Then, not long after that, they got a divorce."

"So what does your father do now?"

"Oh. He takes care of people's gardens. Including Miss Matilde's. Especially, Miss Matilde's."

A door slammed and a stocky gray-haired man in khaki work clothes appeared on the porch of the house. "Sara!" he called. "Sarita! Call your mother. She's been trying to reach you."

"There he is now," Sara said. "Coming, Papá!" she called. And then to Caro, "I'd better go. I'll see you later, huh?"

After Sara left, Caro started back to Las Mariposas but paused where the paths branched. She looked longingly at the wooden bridge and the trees that shaded it, but in a moment trudged resolutely across the little meadow. She had to go to Oak Valley and, although she knew she was a good driver—Ernie had told her so—she would be driving an unfamiliar car and going on new roads to an unfamiliar place. So the sooner it got done, the better.

Chapter 5

🦋 The first thing Caro saw as she neared the house was an old green pickup truck parked by the open garage doors. The second thing was Andy. He was rounding the back of the truck on his way to the rear door of the house. He stopped when he saw her.

"Hi," he called. "Can I bum a ride with you to Oak Valley?" His hands were greasy, his hair disheveled, and his face shone with perspiration.

"Sure," Caro said. "I'll bet you walked up here. Where's your van?"

"At Paley's Pit Stop." Andy pushed a strand of hair away from his forehead. "I had a little trouble. The timing belt."

"That's bad, isn't it?"

"Yeah, but it'll be fixed by the end of the day." He glanced back across the meadow. "I guess you were down to see the shrine."

"How'd you know?"

"Because Sara shows it to everybody. She loves it."

"The creek is pretty nice too. I could learn to love it."

"I know. Brad and I . . ." He didn't finish his thought. Instead he gave his head a sharp little shake and quickened his pace toward the house.

Inside, they found Matilde seated at the table where Caro had left her, papers strewn on the tabletop before her.

She smiled at them and said, "You have a passenger, Caro. Or a driver, if you'd rather."

"Sure. Okay," Caro said, feeling relieved and irritated at the same time. Didn't Matilde trust her driving?

"Here," Andy said and tossed the truck's keys to Caro. "Do you mind stopping at Paley's first?"

"Not if you show me the way."

"You drive. I'll navigate."

The pickup was about the same age as her father's and felt surprisingly familiar. Caro adjusted the mirrors and backed out of the driveway. Silently, she swung the pickup on to the road and headed down the hill the way they had come the day before.

"You drive like a guy," Andy said.

She shrugged. "Why not? I was taught by a guy. A guy named Ernie."

Andy threw her a speculative glance and said, "Turn left on Hill. That's the street by Greg's Market, where I picked you up. Paley's is on the next corner."

Paley's Pit Stop had three pumps, a couple of garage bays, and a crowd of cars scattered throughout the lot. Caro slowed down, then turned into the only available space behind a baker's van.

Immediately, the van's driver sounded his horn, stuck his head out the window and called, "Gimme a break, will ya! I gotta get outta here."

Caro said to Andy, "I'll make a turn around the block, okay?"

"Sure." Andy jumped out of the pickup. "That's all the time I'll need."

Caro drove slowly toward the next corner. She glanced idly at the small buildings she was passing until she saw a sign on one that read, Office of Jerome Poole, Mayor of

Two Sands, California. Then, with a grimace, she looked at the rest of the buildings with more interest. Next to the mayor's office was the city hall and then, at the corner, the Two Sands police station. As she watched, a black car backed out of the narrow driveway between the last two buildings and drove behind her.

Caro turned the corner and headed for the ocean highway. Suddenly, with a loud screeching of brakes, the black car swerved in front of her, blocking her way. She slammed down on the brakes and gave silent thanks when they held. Anger surged through her as she pushed her head out the window, ready to yell, "What's the matter with you?" but stopped when she saw that the car in front of her wasn't all black. It was black and white, and the driver's side door had just swung open. The words she had held back lumped in her throat, almost choking her, as she saw a uniformed policeman step out of the car.

He was tall and thin, with wiry red hair cut short like the bristles of a brush. He marched toward her. "All right, missy," he said, "step on down here."

"What's wrong, officer? I have a driver's license. I can show you."

"Step down here, please," he said firmly.

Caro jumped down from the truck. "What did I do?"

"Come along with me and we'll talk about it."

Caro's heart raced as she took a step alongside the policeman. She stopped abruptly. "Hold it, officer," she said in a loud, but shaky, voice. "Are you arresting me?"

A young man and woman, obviously tourists, who were watching from the sidewalk, nudged one another and grinned.

The policeman's face, under a summer tan, turned a mottled red. "Just come on," he said in a surly tone. "We want to talk to you."

"Can't you talk to me here? I don't want to leave my aunt's truck in the middle of the road like that. Really, it would be better if you'd talk to me here. Unless you're arresting me. And if you are, you have to tell me what for and you have to read me my rights and . . . and I get to make one phone call."

The policeman scowled. "You're all confused, missy," he said. "Come on now."

Caro stamped her foot. "I'm *not* confused!" she shouted. "If you're pulling me in, you've got to tell me why. I learned that in my Civics class."

"Go, girl!" the young woman on the sidewalk called out. The man beside her said, "She could be right, you know, officer. I'm a law student."

"And a witness too," the woman added eagerly.

The officer glanced at the couple on the sidewalk and lowered his voice. "It's the mayor asked me to bring you in. He wants to talk to you, so let's not keep him waiting."

"The *mayor?*" Caro shrieked. "The *mayor?*" A fiery anger coursed throughout her body. "What right does he have to scare me like this? Just because he wants to talk to me? You know what? Tell him I live with my aunt, Matilde Reyes, at Las Mariposas. He can come talk to me there. He knows the way. And, unless you're arresting me, I'm leaving." She glared at the policeman. "Like I said," she blurted out, "unless you're arresting me, I'm leaving." Come on, feet, she ordered silently, move! But her feet weren't moving.

The policeman didn't move either. The expression on his face shifted from surprise to puzzlement. Finally, he seemed to come to a decision. He opened his mouth to speak, but a shout from the corner stopped him.

"Hey! Hey, Caro! What's going on?"

Caro saw Andy loping toward them. She took a deep breath and her heart stopped acting wildly. "Boy, am I glad to see you," she called. "He pulled me over. Not to arrest me, I guess. He says the mayor ordered him to get me."

"What's this all about, Ed?" Andy asked.

The policeman threw a furtive glance at the couple on the sidewalk. They were still watching. "It's all right, Andy," he said and turned to Caro. "We'll just call this a warning today, missy. A warning not to drive without your driver's license because the law's the law, and we don't want anyone forgetting that."

"But I tried to show you my license!" Caro shouted. Then, catching a glance from Andy that clearly said, show it to him, show it to him, she pulled the license from her pocket and held it out for the officer to see.

"All right, all right," the policeman said. "You can go now." He trudged to his black-and-white car, started it and, with a squeal of tires, swung around the corner onto the ocean highway.

The couple on the sidewalk applauded.

"Thanks!" Caro called to them. "Thanks a lot." She headed for the pickup. She paused by the driver's door and said, "You know what, Andy. I think you'd better drive. I'm still boiling. I could blow a gasket."

Andy grinned and, with his chin motioning to the receding couple, said, "Well, *they* thought you were cool. Sure, I'll drive."

They both were silent as they left Two Sands behind them. Caro was still seething. Her mind swirled with scenes in which she got even with Mayor Poole, all of which she shrugged off as implausible. There was no way that she was going to scratch the mayor's eyes out or even sue him. But, as deep breathing and the view of the peaceful blue ocean calmed her down, she started to think more clearly. What was clear was that the mayor was acting pretty stupidly for a supposed adult. What possible difference could *she* make to his plans? Whatever those plans were, they had something to do with making Las Mariposas fail. And how could she stop that? Clearly, the mayor was getting desperate.

There was no doubt that he had wanted to scare her out of Two Sands. All right then. The way to get even with him was to keep him from wearing Tía Matilde down. Great, Caro, she told herself, that's a pretty humongous plan you've laid out for yourself. Maybe it would be easier to scratch the mayor's eyes out. She grinned, almost chuckling, and caught Andy angling a glimpse of her.

She leaned back then, glad that Andy was driving. He has nice hands, she thought, glancing at them on the steering wheel. Even with the grease spots on them. Abruptly, Andy's hands tightened on the wheel until the knuckles showed white and his face, too, tightened, his eyes staring stonily straight ahead.

It took a moment for her to understand what had happened. They had just passed a sharp curve in the road. On that curve, on the side overlooking the ocean, there had been a small collection of vehicles, including a large yellow crane. She felt a cold shiver wriggle up her spine as she realized that that had to be the spot where Brad had gone over the cliff. She sighed, feeling helpless; she wanted to say something, but what?

In another half mile, they turned inland. Andy's hands relaxed on the wheel. "We'll be there in another couple of miles," he said.

Soon the rolling sun-dried hills on each side of the road gave way to groves of fruit trees and to white rail fences that enclosed tree-shaded houses and farm animals. Next, a motel or two appeared and then a sign that announced that Oak Valley had a population of 10,351 and that it was the place "Where Ocean Breezes Come to Rest." The ocean breezes, Caro thought as they entered Oak Valley, are really resting. There's not the tiniest movement of air and it is *hot*. But the town is pretty.

They drove on the main road by several blocks of colorful shops and restaurants that spilled out on to the sidewalks along with pots of azaleas and geraniums. After another few blocks, Andy turned the pickup onto a street called Green.

"Al's Market," he announced as they swung into a large parking lot that had an immense oak tree in its center. "I'll park here and walk to the Ford agency—it's just around the corner—while you get Miss Matilde's groceries."

In less than an hour, Andy and Caro were on their way back to Two Sands. Caro drove. She had been seated in the driver's seat when Andy returned. He said, "Got everything?" and when she nodded, he had jumped into the passenger's seat without another word.

They said very little on the drive back. When she asked Andy if he lived in Two Sands, she was surprised to learn that he was Sara's cousin and that he had lived with her family since he was a child. "My parents died when I was just a little kid, and my aunt and uncle took me in. I think of them as my parents. And why not? That's what they've been to me."

Caro was a little apprehensive when they neared the coastline curve where the cars and the crane were collected, but there was no noticeable reaction from Andy as they passed it. She dropped him off at Paley's Pit Stop.

"Thanks," he said. "See you later."

"Oh?"

"That's right," he said. "You wouldn't know. We're having a little get together tonight in Miss Matilde's garden in honor of Brad."

"A little memorial," she said softly.

"Right. Root beer floats and remembrances."

"Root beer floats," she said with a smile. "I would have liked Brad."

"He loved them." Andy turned abruptly. "I've got to go. Old Paley's giving me a threatening look."

On Caro's ascent to Las Mariposas, her mind was filled with Brad. What had he looked like? What had he been like? Already she was sure that if Andy had loved him, and it was clear that he had, he must have been an all right guy. Because Andy . . . because Andy . . . What did she know about Andy? Well, he liked cats. And *they* liked him. Also he had been kind to the red-haired policeman. All right, she thought as she turned into the Las Mariposas driveway, that should be recommendation enough.

By the time that Caro brought the last load of groceries into the kitchen, she realized that she was starving. Almost two o'clock. Absolutely time for lunch. She wondered if her aunt had had hers.

The door to the hall opened and Mr. Brown pushed his head through. "Thought I heard noises in here," he said. "I came to say goodbye and to thank you for the great breakfast." When she shrugged with an embarrassed little smile, he said, "No, really, it was great." He handed her an envelope. "This is for you."

"For me?" She opened the envelope. It held several ten dollar bills and a business card on which Susan Brown had written, "Thanks for making it possible for us to stay. It was a blessing." Caro looked up at him. "It's so much," she said. "Thank you. But I thought you were staying another night?"

"We wanted to," Mr. Brown said, extending his hands palms up in defeat, "but we were called home. So, off we go."

"I'll come help you with your things."

"No, no. The car is all packed. Goodbye, young lady."

Caro waited until the Browns had driven away before she sought out Matilde. She found her at her desk in the small office next to the kitchen. "Too bad the Browns left," Caro said, "but one good thing. We don't have to change the bed in the Sunrise Room."

"There's another good thing," Matilde said. "Actually, it's two good things. Now we can use the parlor for our remembrance of Brad." She sighed deeply, shook her head and added, "Once we put away the groceries, let's have lunch. But the cats first. Their plates are near the back steps under the overhang. Just rattle the dishes, they'll come running."

Matilde was by the counter, rummaging through the bags of groceries when Caro returned to the kitchen. "Only one of the cats came," she said. "The orange one. Pancake?"

"That's right. Cloud's a wanderer. Sometimes I wish they could be 'inside' cats where I could keep track of them, but with possibly allergic house guests, that would never do. You know, I thought I heard Cloud meowing a bit ago. Oh, well, he'll show up soon. Now, let's eat."

Sara brought candles. And two pictures of Brad. "I came early," she said, glancing at the clock above the fireplace in the parlor. It said eight o'clock. "Mamá and Papá will be here soon."

Caro helped her clear the marble-topped cabinet and place the candles and pictures of Brad on its surface. While Sara went outside to pick a few flowers, Caro looked at the two pictures. One was a head shot, a high school graduation picture, she guessed; the other, a snapshot of Brad and Andy by the tree in the garden. Although the first photograph was wallet size, it was sharp and clear. Brad was a pleasant-looking young man, square-faced, with thick gold hair and eyes that even the small photograph showed to be a deep blue. He was smiling, a small hesitant smile that held a hint of apology.

The other picture showed Brad to be of medium height, stocky, with square shoulders. Andy beside him was a sharp contrast. He was half a head taller than Brad, lean and dark. But the smiles on their faces matched. They were broad and open and filled with high spirits.

Sara returned, and with her came her mother and father. María Ruiz was a short, wiry woman with intelligent dark eyes and short hair that was as black and as thick as Sara's. She acknowledged the introduction to Caro with a nod, a smile, a few words expressing her pleasure and left to find Matilde. Juan Ruiz was gray-haired and clean-shaven. He wore a white short-sleeved shirt and a dark tie above a pair of well-pressed cotton pants. He took Caro's extended hand in a firm grip and pumped it enthusiastically.

"So this is the girl from the city," he said. "Sara says you're a hard worker."

"I am . . . sometimes," Caro said and, at his nod of approval, decided that she liked Juan Ruiz very much.

Andy arrived a few minutes later.

When Caro got up to leave, Sara said, "Oh. You could stay, you know." She glanced at Matilde. "If you want, that is."

"Thanks. Uh . . . uh . . . I don't think so. I didn't know him. This is really for you guys." Juan Ruiz nodded seriously, and Caro shot him a quick little smile and said goodnight.

In her room Caro closed the door softly. She looked at the bed with longing. It's not even dark yet, she thought, and I could crawl into bed this minute. Maybe Papá was right. Maybe I can't handle all this responsibility. I'm really beat. And it isn't just the hard work that's getting to me. It's getting used to the new routine and learning to handle the house guests, even when they're as nice as the Browns. I guess the worst of it is being a part of what's happening to Tía Matilde. That rat fink of a mayor keeps throwing obstacles in her way. My running home scared was supposed to be one of them. How long can she hold out? If only someone knew why he's doing all this, then maybe Tía Matilde would know how to fight back. As it is right now, she would be throwing punches at empty air.

Caro turned down the bedclothes and went to the closet for her pajamas. "Now, where's the light switch?" she mumbled, feeling the surface of the wall with a flat hand. Something moved at her feet, causing her to let out a startled cry. Almost simultaneously she found the light and heard a melancholy meow. Cloud, the gray cat, rubbed himself against her legs and then led the way out of the closet. He sat by the closed hall door and waited with calm confidence for her to open it.

"Hey, you little beast," she said, picking him up and scratching the back of his head, "if you think I'm going to open the door and allow you to wander through the house, you're darned well mistaken." She tiptoed through the kitchen to the outside door. "Out you go."

Caro closed the back door quietly and walked to her bedroom, listening to the hum of voices from the parlor. There was a little burst of laughter and she heard Sara say, "Brad always said that and I always laughed." Good, Caro thought, it's not all tears. And then, because it felt right, she smiled and whispered, "Goodnight, Brad."

Chapter 6

❦ Caro paused by a large willow tree and listened to the soft gurgle of the creek. In another few steps she had left the willow behind and she saw the shrine. Someone had put fresh flowers on the shelf beside the picture of the *virgen*. A narrow little footpath led down to it from the track on which she stood, and she was tempted to spend a few minutes in that quiet place. She debated for a moment about whether or not to go down to it and then, glancing at her watch, decided against it.

When Matilde had told her to take the afternoon off, Caro had agreed to only a couple of hours. Sara and she had worked all morning, leaving the rooms upstairs ready for the six guests who would arrive the next day. Still, before the day was up she planned to clean the parlor; it was obviously worrying Matilde. "Only a couple of hours," Caro had repeated. "I'm going down to Two Sands to see what it's like when I'm not just passing through it."

Matilde laughed. "One hour should be plenty. There's not much to see. Take the pickup if you want."

Caro shook her head. She hadn't told Matilde about the run-in with the policeman. "No, thanks," she had said, "I'm going to take the creek path. Sara says it's a shortcut."

Now, standing above the virgin's shrine, she threw a last look at it and continued down the trail. The path went downhill at a leisurely pace, leaving the trees behind as it followed the bends and turns of the creek. Near a broad swerve of the little stream the path straightened, passing through a pair of squat stone pillars that bore the inscription, "Reyes Ranch, Private Property." Caro continued down the slope and soon found herself at the Old Creek bridge on Hill Street. She leaned on the parapet to reconnoiter.

Although a breeze from the ocean stirred the air, it was hot in the sun. She brought out a Dodger blue baseball cap from her back pocket and pulled it snugly on her head. She breathed deeply. It was good being alone. The walk, with only a few birds and an occasional squirrel to intrude on her privacy, seemed to be just what she needed. In her family she was known as a "loner," which, for some unknown reason, infuriated her. Even as a little kid she had stamped her foot and yelled, "I'm *not* a loner! I just like to be alone sometimes. So leave me alone!"

Now, as she scanned Pier Street with all its shops and people and cars coming and going, she grimaced. By contrast, beyond the busy street, the long, empty wooden pier that jutted into the ocean looked inviting. But she had come to Two Sands to do some "snooping," to see what, if anything, someone might say that would shed some light on Matilde's problem. Of course, it was probably not good sense but dumb curiosity that drove her because who would tell *her* anything?

Directly across from her, facing Hill Street, was a small house that was neatly painted in gray with white trim. As she watched, an old man carrying a ladder appeared from the side of the house. His face was almost hidden by a wide-brimmed straw hat. He leaned the ladder against the house and peered at her.

"You over there," he called. "You're a Dodger fan, eh?"

Caro crossed the street. "Not really," she said when she was near. "I inherited the cap from my kid brother."

"But you love baseball, eh? *Everybody* loves baseball."

"Not me," Caro said with a grin. "Sorry to disappoint you."

The old man stationed the ladder by a vine-covered brick chimney and turned back to her. "*Bueno*," he said with a shrug, "it keeps the sun off your face, no?" He turned and walked to the rear of the house.

Caro walked slowly down Pier Street, stopping to cast brief looks into the stores. Only the barber shop seemed to hold material for a would-be snoop. The barber and the man in the chair were talking seriously. When she heard the mayor's name used, she wished that she could hear more, but since she wasn't a fly on the wall or even a waiting customer, she walked on.

She was at the ocean highway, preparing to cross to the beach, when Andy's van pulled alongside of her.

"Hi, Caro," he called. "What's up?"

"Not much. I thought I'd walk out on the pier."

"Where'd you leave the pickup?"

"At Las Mariposas. I walked."

"Well, if you want a ride back, look for me in Greg's parking lot."

"Thanks. I'll do that."

Andy swung the van around and drove up Pier Street, and Caro crossed the highway to the sand. There, leaning on a large boulder, she removed her shoes and socks, rolled up the legs of her pants and dug into the hot sand with her toes.

She looked back up Pier Street, thinking of Andy. That quick exchange with him had sent a quiver of gladness through her. Of course, she told herself, I know why. I'm in a place filled with strangers, some of them not so nice, and Andy's was a friendly face from home—well, from Las Mariposas, anyway. No wonder I was so glad to see him. She picked up her shoes and headed for the pier.

There she paused and scanned the rough wooden planks. Shrugging, she decided to go on barefoot. The breeze was brisk with a sharp cool edge that was invigorating. She walked the length of the pier slowly, glad for the salty taste of the air and the emptiness that surrounded her.

"You're gonna get splinters," a boy's voice intruded into her supposed solitude.

Caro glanced in the direction of the voice and found a boy, twelve or thirteen, almost hidden by a weathered post that extended above the floor of the pier. He was a scrawny boy dressed in cut-off jeans and worn leather sandals, and, at that moment, he was focused on a taut fishing pole in his hands.

"Did you catch something?" she asked.

"Nah. Probably caught on one of the pilings." He turned to her and grinned. "I never catch anything."

Caro sat down and began putting on her socks and shoes. She looked up at him. "So why do you come here then?"

"To be alone. Nobody comes to the pier anymore. Except you now."

Caro shrugged. "Well, I came here to be alone too. So I guess we're both out of luck."

"Doesn't matter." He reeled in his fishing line. "I gotta go climb a ladder for my uncle, anyway. He's too old now and the ivy's going inside the chimney."

"Weird," she said. "I think I met your uncle just now. The house on Hill Street by the creek bridge?" When he nodded she added, "He sure likes baseball, doesn't he?"

"Nah. He just likes to talk to people. And you're wearing a baseball cap."

"He saw it all right," she said with a little laugh. "And about the ladder. He's got it all set and waiting for you."

The boy nodded and picked up his fishing pole. He muttered a quick goodbye and trodded purposefully toward the town.

Caro walked to the end of the wharf, where she leaned on the wooden rail. She watched the waves build and swell and crash on to the sand. She lingered there for a few minutes, and then, reluctantly, turned and started back to Las Mariposas. At the top of Pier Street she glanced into the parking lot of Greg's Market. She had thought to call, "I'll take you up on that ride," if she saw Andy, but when she did see him, she turned away quickly.

Andy was not alone. With him was Deb, the girl who had tended the market during Brad's funeral. Her red curls glistened in the sun. She was laughing as Andy held her at arm's length. Caro hurried by, but not quick enough to miss Deb's words: "Don't be so hard to please, Andy. Don't you want me to be your girl?"

As Caro turned on to Hill Street, she looked only at the tops of her shoes, the cracks in the sidewalk, and the dusty asphalt of the road. She was across the street and beyond the parapet of the Old Creek bridge before she paused to look back.

The parking lot was hidden from her view, but not the boy from the pier. He was up on the ladder, tugging at the ivy on the chimney of the neat gray house. From his perch near the roof he waved and called, "Hi! Where you going?"

"Up the creek trail."

"Most of that's private property," he called. "Starting at the old stone posts."

"I know. But I won't be trespassing. I'm staying at Las Mariposas."

"Oh, well, sure," the boy said.

"I'm not a guest though," Caro said, sensing the boy's discomfort. "Matilde's my aunt. I'm helping her." She turned and started up the slope. That boy probably wants to talk, she thought, but I don't. I just want to get back. She trudged up the hill with unflagging steps.

Almost before she knew it, she was passing through the stubby stone posts to where the trees began and the path once more paralleled the creek. Here she slowed her pace. Taking a few deep breaths, she felt herself cooling down and calming down. And wondering why she was so upset. It was not any of her business if Andy and that redhead had a thing going. No. It was just that Andy seemed like such a nice guy and that Deb was so . . . she was so . . . darn it! . . . beautiful.

At that thought, her common sense and good humor returned. She shrugged, able to laugh a little at herself. After all, I do have Ernie back home, she thought, even if he isn't exactly a romantic boyfriend, since all he really cares about is cars. In any case, I'm glad I walked down to Two Sands. Maybe I didn't learn anything new about Matilde's problem, not that I'd really expected to, but I enjoyed walking on the pier.

Caro paused at a high point on the path to look down at the dwindling little creek. In the spring, when the snows are melting, she thought, it will probably be filled from bank to bank and then it will really be pretty. She watched a squirrel scamper up a pine tree and then started walking once more.

In another few minutes she saw ahead of her the small bridge that led to Matilde's meadow. As she neared it, she was surprised to find the old man from the Hill Street house crossing over it toward her. He carried his straw hat held loosely in his hand, exposing a full head of gray hair. His black eyes were sharp and intelligent.

He waved the hat at her. "¡Hola!" he called. "And where have you been?"

"To the pier," she said and was about to add, "but it's not really your business, is it?" when the friendly, expectant look on his face caused her to bite back the words. "He just likes to talk to people," the boy on the pier had said. So, instead, she added, "It was nice by the ocean. And where have you been?"

"To visit the walnut groves," he said as he stepped on to the path. "Poor, poor trees."

"Sara says they're not very healthy."

"And Sara is right. Long ago I told Don Armando that they would never come back. Of course, I was only a boy then, and he paid no attention to me. If my father had been alive Don Armando might have listened, but as it was . . ." The thought hung unfinished in the afternoon air. "And, later," the old man continued, "when I knew him as an adult, he respected my skills as a carpenter—I built the virgin's chapel and a few things in the house—but he never conceded that he had been wrong about the land."

"Don Armando. You mean Matilde's grandfather?".

"Her grandfather, yes. And more than that. Doña Luisa and Don Armando were like mother and father to those girls. They brought them here from Mexico after an incident that left the girls' parents dead."

"How awful." Caro added, "So the girls you're talking about were Matilde and Mercedes."

"Ah," the old man said, "you know the story."

"No, no. Only that Mercedes is my mother. I'm Carolina Torres. I'm visiting my Tía Matilde."

The old man bent his head in acknowledgment and said, "I'm Pedro Jiménez, señorita. I'm glad to know you. So you're Mercedes' daughter. I knew her only a little. She went down to the city to marry a man Don Armando disapproved of and she wasn't allowed back."

Caro's face grew hot. "My father's a good man," she burst out. "Don Armando must have been a hard-headed old man."

"Oh, yes. He was a stubborn one . . ."

"So is my mother," Caro interrupted. "She probably put her foot down when he . . ." She stopped and grinned. "And so am I. I guess it's in the genes."

"So I tell myself," Pedro Jiménez said, a twinkle in his eye.

"Well, now I know why we never came to visit Tía Matilde, even though my mother and she stayed in touch. Thank you for telling me. I always wondered. Well, goodbye, señor. I've got to go now." At the other end of the bridge Caro swung around and said, "I'm sorry about the walnut trees."

The old man shook his head. "It's not only the trees. Half of this hill was poisoned by chemicals used by a pottery plant that stood here before I was born. When Don Armando bought the house, my mother told him what she knew and warned him not to buy the land north of the little meadow, but, as you now know, he was not a man given to listening to others. Well, he paid for it. The groves never did well. And when he tried to sell some of the land, no one would buy it. How he made a living no one knows." He paused and grinned. "Go, young lady. I'll talk on and on if you don't."

"I'm going," Caro said with a little laugh. "Goodbye."

She went through the stand of eucalyptus trees and started across the golden meadow. Someone was standing by the gate to Las Mariposas. It was Andy. He held the gate open for her.

"I saw you go by Greg's," he said, "but by the time I could get away, you were gone. Why didn't you wait for me?"

"Because you were busy."

"Busy. Yeah, I sure was. Actually, I could've used your help. Deb gets sort of enthusiastic around guys."

"All guys? Really?"

"Yeah. Brad and I had a thing we did. We kept track of who she came on to the most. Brad would've won, hands down, but . . . well . . . now I'm getting more attention."

"And you don't like it at all, do you?" Caro said, shaking her head slowly. "Are you going to try to sell me the Brooklyn Bridge next?"

Andy laughed. "She *is* pretty."

"*Pretty?* Come off it, Andy. She's absolutely gorgeous."

"Yeah, I'll give her that. But not much more." He grinned at her. "After all, she can't drive a stick shift."

"Poor baby," Caro said and smiled up at him, noting how nicely the sun shone on his dark brown hair. "I've got to go in now."

"I'm coming too," Andy said and, together, they walked to the house.

Inside they found Matilde in her office, seated in front of the computer.

Caro said, "I'm back. And ready to clean the parlor. If you'll tell me which wax to use."

"Don't bother," Matilde interrupted in a listless tone. "Even if we managed tomorrow's breakfast, the next three days will be impossible. I don't know what I was thinking. I'm figuring out what it's going to cost me to do it because I'm going to have to cancel."

Chapter 7

"No," Caro said. "No, Tía Matilde. Please, don't."

Matilde looked up at her and shook her head. "I'm afraid I don't have any choice."

"Why?" Andy asked. "Did something else happen?"

"A small thing, yes. But sometimes it's a small thing that breaks the camel's back or foot or whatever. One of tomorrow's guests called and insisted on a cholesterol-free, or almost cholesterol-free breakfast. I told her that wouldn't be a problem. I hung up, and, as soon I did, I realized. No problem? What was I thinking? Of course, it's a problem. We planned three buffet breakfasts for the weekend: egg, cheese, and ham strata on Friday, *huevos rancheros* in a chafing dish on Saturday, and salmon, mushrooms and capers in a rich cream sauce on Sunday. So what could she eat?"

Caro said, "But, Tía Matilde, there'll be all the other stuff. You know, fruit and . . . and there's some low-fat yogurt in the fridge and . . ."

"And little boxes of cold cereal? No, honey, we couldn't do that. The reputation of our B&B would be ruined."

"Miss Matilde," Andy said softly. "What will happen to your reputation if you cancel these people with less than a day's notice?" Matilde looked at him as she took a long, deep breath but said nothing.

Caro sat down on a chair behind Matilde and said, "Did you know that my father has high cholesterol? He won't take any pills, so my mother really has to watch his diet." Matilde swung her office chair around to face her, a frown growing on her face. "Yes," Caro went on, "and did you know that my mother is a great cook?"

"All right, honey," Matilde said patiently, "what are you trying to tell me?"

"That my mother makes the best thin little pancakes for Papá—I guess they're called crepes—made with egg whites and filled with absolutely great stuff like green peppers and zucchini in a tomato sauce and low-fat cheese sprinkled over them. Or she fixes cut up fruit in a non-fat yogurt mixture that makes you drool, it's so good. That's only for Sundays. Papá gets hot oatmeal for breakfast on the other days."

"Ratatouille," Matilde offered.

"What? Oh, yes, the tomato stuff," Caro said. "And if you have a small non-stick frying pan, I can make those pancakes and I can get the recipes for the fillings from Mamá."

"Caro, Caro, Caro," Matilde said, with a shake of her head. "You don't give up, do you? If you're in the kitchen making crepes for Mrs. Groman, who will serve her? And the coffee? And who will keep the buffet presentable? You know Sara's too shy to deal with people."

"I will," Andy said. "I'll wear my best white shirt and you can check my fingernails to see if they're presentable."

Matilde sighed. "It seems to me that I've already had a conversation very much like this with Caro and Sara. And now it's Caro and you who are figuring out ways to save me. It'll soon be all your family helping me, Andy. First, it was María, Sara, and your father and now . . ." She held her hands out as if in defeat. "I can't let you do it, Andy. I know how much every dollar you earn in that taxi of yours helps toward your college plans. No, I can't let you do it. Besides, you still have to deliver groceries for Greg."

Andy was silent for a moment and then he said, "Not anymore. Greg let me go yesterday. I could tell he felt bad doing it, but, you know, he had to."

Caro gasped. "The mayor again? It's not fair! How can he do that?"

Matilde said, "I'm starting to wonder where this is going next? And what's this all about?"

"There's more, Miss Matilde," Andy said. "I can't drive people in my so-called taxi anymore either. Not without a business license that would take weeks to get, not to mention that it would cost a fortune. So, you see, I'm totally free and it would be awesome to thwart the mayor at whatever he's up to around here."

Caro looked from Andy to Matilde, thinking, how did it happen that in just three days these two people have become so important in my life? And how did it happen that I can hate someone so much, someone I've never seen before? She took a deep breath and let it out slowly. If it takes the rest of the summer, she thought, I'm going to help Tía Matilde find out what Mayor Poole's plotting. Even if he is a big shot.

"What I think he's up to," Matilde said, as if reading Caro's mind, "is the house. He wants the house, and I have no idea why. He hated it when he lived here. When we were married he spent a great deal of time trying to persuade me to tear it down and get rid of the groves. So that he could build a world-class golf course. That was his dream. But, of course, I gave him an absolute no. Then I learned that the experts he'd called in supposedly to check the groves were really golf course designers. What they told him was that there was no hope of growing the kinds of grasses and other plants needed for a golf course on most of this land. They told him to forget it. He would get in a rage for days. I learned all this from other sources, of course. Then, several years after our divorce, he started hounding me to sell him the house. And when I wouldn't, he started causing trouble for me. Sometimes I think that's why he ran for mayor. Being mayor of Two Sands doesn't carry much prestige or money, but it does allow you to nose into things and also to pull strings, as we've seen. He probably figures that if I can't pay the property taxes, he'll pick the house up for a song.

"Well, enough of that. I'm talking too much. All right, Andy, you're on. Caro, call your mother. From the look on your faces I'd say you're ready to do battle." She smiled. "I guess our weapons can be crepes and ratatouille." Then Matilde added, "I promise not to lose heart again. Not with you two on my side."

Sara came to Las Mariposas late that afternoon and, together, Caro and she made a small amount of ratatouille and a few crepes that the three of them had for dinner.

"They're not too bad for a practice run, are they?" Caro asked. "Maybe a little less onion."

"All right," Matilde said, "a bit less onion. Although they're practically perfect now. You're going to be as good a cook as your mother."

The next day, as planned, Andy came at one o'clock to be on hand when the guests arrived. After Matilde greeted them, Andy carried their suitcases up the stairs while Caro and Sara showed them to their rooms. He stationed the guests' cars for them in the marked slots at the side of the house and answered their questions about the town.

"There are several good restaurants down by the ocean and also in Oak Valley," he said to the Gromans, adding with a grin, "but not much night life."

Mr. Groman, a stocky man with a well-trimmed beard on his full face, nodded and shrugged, then suddenly said, "Do you play cards, young man?"

"Not with strangers, sir," Andy replied seriously.

Mr. Groman threw his head back and burst into a brief loud laugh. "Don't let this one get away, young lady," he said to Caro who was standing at the foot of the stairs. "This one's a keeper."

"I'll remember that," Caro said and felt herself blushing. Luckily, Andy was bent over, picking up some papers Mrs. Groman had dropped, and she escaped to the kitchen before he had straightened up.

Late that afternoon, with Matilde perched on a high stool at the kitchen counter and Sara and Caro bouncing between the refrigerator and the stove, the preparation for the breakfast buffet was completed.

Andy, who apologized thoroughly for not staying to help in the kitchen, had left to take one of his "regulars" to see her doctor in Oak Valley. He assured Matilde that the mayor wouldn't get after him, because it had been decided between him and his regular customer that this trip, no matter what it cost, would be reported, if it was necessary, as a favor from a friend. "There are several ways to skin a cat, aren't there?" he said with a grin and he hurried out of the kitchen, biting into a strawberry he had swiped from a pile on the counter.

Now, with the food disposed of and the dining table ready to be set quickly, Sara went home and Matilde, to her room to rest. Caro was alone and, suddenly, feeling restless and a little bit homesick. She went to the back door, planning to sit quietly in the back garden but found that four of the guests had taken over the table and chairs under the elm.

Ignoring the unreasonable annoyance she felt, she settled for second best, the small garden on the east side of the house. A cobblestone path that led to the backyard hugged the house. Mr. Ruiz had planted a colorful garden between it and the stone fence that half hid the guests' parked cars. Late summer flowers surrounded a patch of green lawn. Banking the front gate at the far end of the garden were two earthenware jars overflowing with pink ivy geraniums. In the center of the lawn a wooden bench sat in the lattice-like shade of a slender plum tree. And, half hidden under a low-growing shrub, Pancake watched lazily as Caro stepped through the French doors in the dining room and headed to the bench.

This is what it is to be happily tired, Caro thought, leaning back on the bench. It's being tired because you've done something worthwhile. Like it's not plain, ordinary cooking and cleaning, it's cooking and cleaning that are going to help Tía Matilde beat the mayor at whatever game he's playing. It's scary though. Maybe I *have* assumed too much responsibility. Twice I talked Tía Matilde into not canceling her guests, once with Sara's help, the other with Andy's. Still, Tía Matilde had seemed so lost, so kind of helpless. Somebody had to do something. So I did.

Caro grimaced. Probably Tía Matilde had been feeling lost and helpless when the mayor talked her into marrying him. Her own mother would have sent him packing. Nobody could talk her mother into having a cup of coffee much less into marrying, or not marrying. No wonder Don Armando had banished her from Las Mariposas. She had probably stamped her foot and told him where to get off when he had forbidden her to marry the man she had learned to love. How could the two sisters be so different? At that thought Caro burst into quiet laughter. Easy, she told herself. It's true that Luisa and I both like to cook—actually she just likes to bake—but that's where any similarity ends. She likes soft sweaters and jeweled sandals and I like sweatshirts and duck-billed caps. She likes romance novels and I'll read everything but romance novels. When we were kids she begged for ballet lessons and I chose karate. How different can you get? Oh, well, we both like to surf the Internet, but I'll bet she never stamped her foot at anyone.

Different as they were, she missed Luisa. If she hadn't left her cell phone in Angela's room, she would call her sister right this minute. But any good intentions would have to wait. She was too tired to walk all the way into the house.

Caro stayed in the side garden doing nothing—unless talking to an unresponsive cat was considered something—for another half hour. She rose and stretched. It was while she was stretching that her eyes focused on a movement under a tree in the field behind the parked cars. When the movement resolved itself into a person and that person stepped cautiously from the shade into a band of sunlight, Caro drew in her breath sharply. She knew that glinting red hair. Deb. It was Deb. What was she doing skulking around Las Mariposas? Caro moved to the fence where, half hidden by the top of a guest's SUV, she waited to see what the redhead was doing.

Deb scanned the house thoroughly, then took a few guarded steps into the open field before pausing to check out the house once more. Caro grinned. What was that girl trying to do? Catch Andy unaware? Deb took a few more stealthy steps then stopped and peered slowly along the length of the fence. No, it was more than peering, she was squinting, her eyes pulled into slits as she tried to make out something that escaped her at that distance. With an impatient shake of her head, Deb straightened up and started forward. What her intention might have been was not made clear because at that same moment the four B&B guests who had been under the elm appeared from the front of the house, talking and laughing. When they saw Deb they smiled and waved, and Deb, with a toss of the head, waved back. She bent over, picked up something from the ground and walked slowly toward the oak tree.

Caro waved at the guests.

"On your break?" one of the men asked and she nodded.

The two women leaned over the fence. One, a plump little woman with wide-set blue eyes, said, "What a darling garden. Is it for guests too?"

"Absolutely," Caro said as if she owned the place. "Those doors lead to the dining room."

When the four guests had driven off in their cars and the parking area was empty, she cupped her mouth with her hands and shouted, "Hey, Deb, where are you?"

Just as she had expected, there was no answer.

She turned to go inside and then, with a sly grin, she swung around. "Hey, Deb!" she shouted again. "What the heck was that all about?"

There was no answer. Only the sound of a squirrel scurrying across the field.

Chapter 8

🦋 When Caro awakened on Monday morning, she gave the silent alarm clock on the bedside table a snubbing glance and settled back under her summer blanket for a few more minutes of rest. The long weekend was over! In her mind the past three, no, more like three-and-a-half, days were a blur of cleaning guests' bedrooms, cooking, washing up, and serving breakfasts. Mornings had been the worst. It had been a hop, skip, and jump from the early morning coffee in the parlor until the upstairs bedrooms were done.

If Sara and she were angels, as Matilde had said, then María was the best of all angels. She had cleaned the bathrooms and washed all the sheets and towels. The downstairs rooms received a quick vacuuming and dusting and after that came a couple of blissful free hours. And they all had needed them. Here and there amidst the hard work there had been some laughs and some pleasant moments. For instance, Mrs. Groman absolutely loved the crepes and begged for the recipes. Matilde had given Caro all the credit for both the crepes and the fillings, so there had been an extra large tip for Caro when the Gromans left.

Caro stretched contentedly. Monday afternoon and Tuesday breakfast, she was sure, would prove to be a piece of cake. Only two women, both over middle age, Matilde had said, were expected, and they were to share the Meadow Room. Better yet, they had requested an early breakfast. They were amateur geologists and they planned to spend the day tramping in the Robles Hills to collect evidence that would prove something or other to their colleagues. They had been at Las Mariposas before, and Matilde liked them. She liked them because they were usually gone all day after a simple breakfast of oatmeal and overdone eggs and bacon. She also liked them because they were pleasant and kind and loved her two cats.

Caro, with the prospect of a not-so-busy day, decided that right after breakfast she would walk down to the ocean again. Matilde was taking advantage of the light day. Andy and she had left for Oak Valley to keep an appointment with her orthopedic doctor.

Caro hurried through breakfast, anticipating her walk. One look in her closet changed her mind. She had run out of clean clothes. Maybe before lunch, she could sneak her own clothes into the washer between the loads of sheets and towels. So at ten thirty that morning, with a smiling María having assured her that the next load of sheets would be the last, Caro pulled her clothes out of the closet and dumped them on her bed. It was when she was emptying out the pockets of a pair of jeans that a small object flew on to the floor and rolled with annoying speed toward the far corner of the room.

"Oh, blast it!" she fumed. "Now where did it go?" It was her lucky coin, a bicentennial silver dollar that her father had given her. On the day that she left Los Angeles, she had slipped it into her pocket as she left the house. Well, she thought as she got down on her hands and knees to look for it, at least I didn't drop it in the bus or on the highway. But *where* is it?

After looking along the back wall and lifting the edges of the throw rugs, she determined that it had to be under the roll top desk. She dragged the old swivel chair out of the kneehole and, once again on her hands and knees, crawled into the kneehole to retrieve the silver dollar. It was on its edge, leaning against the back panel of the desk. She edged farther into the cramped space and reached for the silver disc only to push it under a loosened strip of molding. It lay flat now, just out of reach. Lying on her belly she squeezed a bit farther into the kneehole, but found that her arms were either too long, too short, or not jointed in the right places for her to reach the dollar. She squeezed out and tried another tactic. This time lying on her back, she slid into the opening of the old desk and found that by swinging her left arm across her chest she could reach the silver coin. When she finally had it in her hand, she started to push out of the uncomfortable space but stopped when her eyes caught something in the left corner above her. A single sheet of paper hung from the top drawer on the left side of the kneehole. It was pressed loosely between the backs of the drawers and the panel that fully covered the back of the desk. The sheet looked as if it had slid out of the top drawer and had been held there by some roughness or stickiness of the wood.

With the back of her hand pressed against the panel, Caro stretched her fingers upward and grasped a corner of the sheet. It came easily. Something of Angela's, she thought as she slid out of the kneehole and, still sitting on the floor, looked at the paper in her hand. It was not Angela's. It was written in Spanish and, according to Matilde, Angela did not speak Spanish, nor read it, of course.

The handwritten words at the top of the page said, "*. . . And so, my dear, I have done what I could do to secure your future.*" This was obviously the continuation of a letter. She flipped the sheet over and found that the back was blank. She went on reading.

"*I could see no other way to do that and protect myself. And, because you are u kind, loving person, I know that you will forgive a frightened old man, one who lived with the terror that his enemies would discover where he was hidden. One thought has consoled me as I write this. If you did not live with wealth in my lifetime, you will when I am gone. My bequest to you, I assure you, will have grown in value over the years. Share it if you will. I have made no restrictions against that because a gift is not a gift when given with ties.*

"*Well, there it is. I have reread the above instructions and find them clear and specific. You will have no trouble following them. And after having written this, I can spend my remaining time in peace. I have provided well for you. Think kindly of me. P. *"

Caro looked quickly through all the drawers and under the roll top; there was no more of the letter there. She read the page she had once more. To whom had it been written? And when? It might have been stuck in between the panels of the old desk for a hundred years. Still, the paper wasn't too yellowed. Maybe being in such a protected place, away from the light, had kept it from drying out and yellowing. Caro shook her head. What did she know about how paper aged? Absolutely nothing. So she might as well stop all the guesswork. She had to show it to Matilde, of course. But if it was a letter for Matilde, wouldn't it drive her crazy not to have the other sheets, not to know what this was all about? The last thing

Matilde needed right now was another mystery hassling her. The mayor's doings were enough.

As Caro debated the question, she heard Sara's cascading laughter coming from the kitchen. Good. She needed someone to bat this around with. Just maybe Sara would know who "P" was. She jumped up, scanned the room, and found just what she needed. A large, glossy food magazine lay on a table by the television. Carefully, she slid the handwritten sheet between the pages of the magazine, tucked it under her arm and, hugging the pile of clothes from the bed against her chest, headed for the laundry room.

She was surprised to find that it was Andy, not María, with whom Sara was laughing.

"Hi, guys," Caro called as she dumped her bundle of clothes by the washing machine. "Where's Matilde? And how is she?"

"At Gloria's Beauty Shop. Her cast has been replaced by a lighter one and she's feeling like celebrating. It's great to see her in a happier mood," Andy replied.

"What are *you* doing here?" Sara asked. "I thought you were going for a walk."

Caro shrugged. "Me too. Until I found nothing but dirty clothes in my closet. So I figured maybe I should wash them. Look, you guys," she added. "Do you have a minute? I've got something to show you."

"We have something to show you too," Sara said with a giggle. "Have you seen Cloud?"

"No. Why?"

"He's decorated his front paws," Andy said. "The pads now have green and yellow markings and he's going crazy trying to wash them off."

"What's he gotten into?"

Andy shrugged. "Who knows? Okay, your turn for show and tell. I have time. I don't have to pick Matilde up for an hour or so."

"All right," Caro said, handing the magazine to Sara over the room partition, "look at what's on page seventy while I get my clothes into the washing machine."

"What? A recipe?" Sara said. "Oh, I see, this note, you mean." She sat at the small breakfast table to read the letter. Andy read it over her shoulder.

Except for the sound of water filling the washer, there was silence in the room for the following few minutes. Then Andy spoke.

"Where'd you get this?"

Caro held up the silver dollar. "I was chasing after this in my room a while ago," she said, "when it rolled under the old desk." Then she went on to tell them where and how she had found the sheet.

"It's part of a letter," Sara said.

"And it's in Spanish," Andy added with a teasing grin.

"All right, smarty," Sara responded, "it's obvious that it's a letter. But who wrote it? And who was it written to?"

"Who knows?" Andy said. "But the fact that it's written in Spanish is a clue. And where it was found. Matilde says that that old roll top desk has been around ever since she can remember, but who knows who it belonged to before that."

Caro pulled out the other chair at the breakfast table and sat. She shook her head. "I was hoping you guys would have answers, but all you have are the same questions I do. Who wrote it? Why? Who was supposed to get it?"

Andy said, "Maybe the person it was written to *did* get it."

"Well, then, she or he lost the last page 'cause we have it," Sara said.

Caro said, "My question is, is it Matilde's?"

Sara shook her head vigorously. "No, no, couldn't be. She'd be rich according to the letter. And is Matilde rich?"

"No way," Caro said.

Andy, who was now sitting on the floor, leaning against the island counter, frowned and said, "There's no use stewing about it now. Matilde will know."

"Do we have to show it to her?" Caro asked. Sara and Andy looked at her in surprise. "I mean right away," she added quickly. "Look, Andy, you said she seemed almost happy today, and that's a change, isn't it? So what will happen if we show her this thing? She'll have a new problem to worry about."

"But what if it's for her after all?" Sara asked, a frown of concentration on her face. "No," she answered herself, "that would make the problem worse, wouldn't it? She'd figure that that money, or jewels, or whatever, would solve all her problems, wouldn't she? And it would be terrible not to know where to find it."

"That's how I see it," Caro said. "How about you, Andy?"

Andy frowned again. "Say you don't show her the letter for a few days, what good will that do?" He stared at Caro for a minute and then, with a questioning tilt of his head, said, "Unless you're thinking that we can find the rest of the letter, or somehow, during that time, find out what it said. Are you?"

"Am I what? Oh, thinking that. Well, yes, I was. I am. Because if we do find out something about it, look how great that would be for Matilde, and if we don't, what harm was there in waiting?"

"None," Andy said, "except that this is Matilde's house and anything in it belongs to her. Hanging on to that old letter is like borrowing somebody's car without asking."

"Come on, Andy," Caro said, "it's not at all like that. She'd miss her car, but who's going to miss something they don't even know exists? Besides, maybe the rest of the letter is in a desk drawer; I haven't looked thoroughly yet. And, if that's the case, we'll give the whole thing to her right away."

Sara took a deep breath, exhaled and said, "Andy, you know Caro's right. We should look around a bit before we bother Matilde with this letter."

"What's a *bit*?" Andy asked. "A day or two?"

"Or three," Caro answered, "but not much longer."

"Okay then," Andy said with a grin. "Where do we begin looking?"

Chapter 9

🦋 They began with the roll top desk. They walked into Caro's room and up to the desk, where Andy crawled into the kneehole and out again "Not much room to move around down there," he said, "but I guess I see where you found the letter."

Caro said, "It must have slipped over the back of this drawer." She pulled open the first of three drawers on the left side of the kneehole. It was shallow, with a built-in wooden set of concave slots for pencils and pens at the front, the remaining section was deep enough for a ream of paper. They took turns looking at the drawer, feeling where the sheet might have slid over and then agreeing that, yes, that was what must have happened. "Maybe," Caro added, "whoever mailed or delivered that letter didn't realize, or forgot, that there was a second page."

"Yeah," Andy said, "there are all sorts of possibilities."

"Let's look at the rest of the desk," Sara said. "Who knows what we'll find."

"Sure," Caro said and she rolled up the top of the desk to disclose a series of cubbyholes and three tiny drawers above a scratched and ink-stained writing area. Both the cubbyholes and the small drawers were empty. The drawers on either side of the kneehole held a couple of rusty paper clips and bits of dust lint.

"I guess Angela doesn't use this desk to write her letters," Caro said.

"She uses the computer," Sara said, "even for her snail mail."

Andy was bent over the desk, looking at the mechanism that rolled the top. "This looks really old," he said. "Bet it's a real antique. In fact, now that I think of it, Brad once told me that his dad thought it was probably worth a couple of thousand or more. Anyway, it's valuable. That's probably why Angela doesn't touch it."

"Makes sense," Caro said. "Why don't you ask Matilde about that? You know, off-hand like. Maybe you could say I was asking you about it."

Andy grinned at her. "I like your leadership qualities," he said. "Okay, Chief, I'll ask her. But, remember, my heart's not exactly in this."

Sara aimed a reproachful look at him and said, "Phooey. I'll ask our parents. Papá especially. They might know who lived here before Mr. Reyes. And whoever *they* were, maybe they owned this desk."

Caro smiled at her. "That's a good idea. I wonder who I could ask about the desk. Do you guys have any—oh, I know. I'll ask the old man who lives in the house at the foot of the creek road. He seems friendly and willing to talk; he knew Mr. Reyes."

"He'll talk your arm off," Andy said. "Well, I've got to get going." At the hall door he turned and sent them a mischievous grin. "Don't solve the mystery while I'm gone."

Sara threw a paper clip at him but missed.

Twenty minutes later Andy brought Matilde back to Las Mariposas. Her thick gray hair had been trimmed and its natural curl fell softly around her ears. She looked renewed, refreshed, and almost happy as she stepped into the kitchen through the back door.

Caro, who was at the dryer folding the rest of her clothes, looked up and said, "You look great, Tía Matilde. How do you feel?"

"Lighter," Matilde said, hobbling over to a chair. "With this lighter cast I'll be able to manage beautifully with my cane. Isn't that something?"

"Hey," Caro said, "congratulations."

"Thanks," Matilde replied. "I'm getting better by the minute, but I'd still better have a rest before our guests arrive. It was quite a morning."

Caro gathered up her clean clothes and glanced at the clock on the stove. "María said she'd be returning just about now. When she does come, do you mind if I take an hour off? I'd like to go for a walk."

"Go, by all means. Take your time."

Within ten minutes, Caro was on her way to see Mr. Jiménez. As she crossed the meadow toward the stand of eucalyptus trees, she felt even more convinced that the decision not to tell Matilde about the letter was right. Today Matilde's face had lost the stiff look of tension, pain, and sadness that had been there before. Yes, Caro thought, we couldn't tell her now. Maybe that letter will turn out to be a dud and, if that's so, all the more reason not to dump it on her.

At the edge of the creek trail a squirrel swished his luxurious tail when Caro came near and then sat motionless as she went by. Above her a pair of small brown birds flew in quick darts from tree to tree, chirping in agitation at her presence. Except for the squirrel and the busy birds, the creek road seemed uninhabited. She stopped at the Guadalupe shrine and when she noticed that fresh flowers were there again, she wondered who brought them. She took a deep breath, enjoying the dry musty smell of the

piled leaves at her feet, enjoying the barely audible trick-
ling sound of the creek and the contentment of being
alone. This, she thought, as she started down the path
again, is almost as good as sitting under the tree in my
backyard alone with a book.

Her solitude did not last long. In just a few more steps,
where the path curved slightly, she saw a girl with a cap
ful of red curls coming up the path. It was Deb. A thin,
paper-wrapped package hung from Deb's hand as she
walked up the hill. There was something in her determined stride and the frown on her face that prompted
Caro to hide behind a bush at the side of the trail. When
Deb came near her hiding place, Caro held her breath, let-
ting it out slowly once Deb had passed. Caro slipped back
on the path. Deb could no longer be seen, but her familiar
floral fragrance still clung to the air. She's so pretty, Caro
thought, so sweet smelling, but today she looks pretty
menacing. I wonder what she's up to. Maybe she's one of
those people who gets mad at the world easily. She looks
as if she's going somewhere to do something. And not
necessarily something good. Stop it, Caro, she scolded
herself. Don't let your imagination run away with you.
She's probably on her way to return something to Mrs.
Ruiz or to whoever lives beyond the walnut grove. In any
case, it's none of your business.

Within minutes Caro was at the bottom of the hill,
across the creek bridge and knocking on the front door of
Mr. Jiménez's trim gray house. The boy from the pier
answered the door. He was wearing cut-off jeans like the
ones he had worn the day she met him and the same
leather sandals. His brown eyes widened in surprise.
"Hey," he said. "It's you. What do you want?"

"Hey, yourself," Caro returned. "I'd like to talk to your uncle. Is he here?"

"Yes, he's here. He's out back." He pushed open the screen door and slid out. "Come on," he said.

She followed him along the side of the house and into a backyard that was shaded by a large evergreen elm. Mr. Jiménez stood by a wooden pole to which was attached a small blue birdhouse, peaked roof and all.

"Señorita," he said, turning, "to what do we owe the pleasure of your visit?" He removed his hat and smiled at her with genuine warmth as he spoke. She smiled too, enjoying his old-fashioned courtesy.

"My curiosity," she said. "I'd like to ask you a few questions."

"Ah-h," he said. "About your grandfather?"

"Actually, he's my great grandfather, but, no, not exactly about him. More about the people who lived in that house before him."

"*Bueno*," he said and moved to a pair of wooden chairs under the tree. "Please sit down." When she was seated he said, "I was still a boy when there were other people in that house, so I know very little. I do know that it was an old couple named James who lived there, and when Mrs. James died, the old man sold the house and moved away. But who knows where?" He grinned. "I was much more interested in the new people, especially the pretty young ladies."

The boy, who was standing by the birdhouse, snickered. "Yeah, yeah, Uncle Pete, you must've had some cool moves then."

"You're probably right," Mr. Jiménez said good-naturedly.

Caro smiled at the boy and turned back to his uncle. "Maybe you'd know this: Did the old roll top desk that's in the house now belong to the Jameses?"

"No, that old desk belonged to us. My father bought it for my mother. Where he got it I do not know. But I remember well that the desk was large, too large for our small rooms. Besides, my mother, bless her soul, did not want a desk, she wanted a piano. *Dios mío*, the house got so dark with that desk in the house. So much so that when Don Armando expressed an interest in it, my father gladly sold it to him. Not long after that we acquired a small piano and there was sunlight in our house again. The short answer is, no, it did not belong to Mr. James."

Caro said, "Well, that settles that. It really *is* big, isn't it? It has so many little drawers and cubbyholes."

There was a twinkle in the old man's eye as he said, "But no secret compartments, I can guarantee that. For the short time we had it, I wasted a lot of time looking for one. Day in and day out, I would tinker with that desk. My father became exasperated with me and, with a measure in hand, showed me the impossibility of a secret compartment. It was a lesson well taught and one that has helped me in my carpentry. Still, it was difficult to learn that not every old desk had secrets. *Bueno*, I hope I haven't spoiled a treasure hunt for you and Sara."

"No, you haven't spoiled anything for us. We stumbled into something that made us curious, but it has nothing to do with a secret compartment."

Mr. Jiménez raised his eyebrow but said nothing. She smiled at him, wondering if she should tell him more, and then decided against it. He turned to the boy. "Antonio," he said, "bring our guest some of those nice grapes Mrs. Delgado gave us."

"No, no, Antonio," Caro said quickly. "I can't stay."

"That's okay," the boy said. "I won't bring the grapes, but you gotta call me Tony."

"It's a deal, Tony," Caro said. And to Mr. Jiménez, "Thank you for telling me about the desk." She hesitated for a moment and then added, "Just one more question. Does Deb, you know the girl that helps in Greg's Market, go up and down the creek trail a lot?"

"Yeah," Tony said. "I think she's after Andy. It used to be Brad, but—"

"Antonio!" his uncle called. "¡Basta!"

"I know, I know, Uncle Pete, you don't like me to say things like that, but it's true, anyway."

Mr. Jiménez sighed and, turning his attention away from the boy, said, "You didn't know young Brad, he was a good boy."

"He must've been," Caro said. "So many nice people like him. Thank you again. I'll tell Sara about the desk."

"Wait, please," Mr. Jiménez said, rising. He plucked a small rose from a trellis on the garage wall and handed it to her. "This is a Cecil Bruner, an old-fashioned little rose that I love. Go with God, young lady."

Caro thanked him and started up the creek path, ignoring the pleasant sea breeze that moved lightly through the trees and the lively chatter of birds darting from tree to tree. Her mind was busy with what she had learned about the desk. Not just its ownership. Even more important was the fact that Mr. Jiménez and his father, "with a measure," had examined that desk from top to bottom. They had found no secret compartment and, obviously, no hanging letters. Almost immediately after that they had sold it. So, of course, that all meant that the letter must have been written by her disagreeable great grandfather.

She was not surprised. Somehow she had known it all along. But where was the first page of the letter? And what was the fortune that he couldn't have spent before? It had to be something that could be traced to him. And he obviously didn't want to be found, so how could he use it? Maybe it was stocks or bonds or some other fancy kind of investment. But what did she know? She was so lost in her thoughts that she was at the Guadalupe shrine before she knew it. And there, sitting on a log and staring into space, was Andy.

She stopped just above the shrine, not sure of what to do. Andy's thoughts definitely were far, far away and, more than that, it was clear that they were sad. He looks so miserable, she thought. I've never seen him look like that before. Her impulse was to run down and comfort him, but her good sense stopped her. Comfort him? Sure, sure, she told herself. Who do you think you are, Caro, Mother Teresa?

It was at that moment that Andy looked up and saw her. "Hi, Chief," he called. "I came down to meet you."

"Really?" What made the sea breeze warmer? And its touch more velvety on her face? She shook her head as if to dismiss her thoughts and said, "Well, you didn't look too happy about it."

"That's your fault," he said. "If you'd gotten here sooner, my mind wouldn't have drifted off to unhappy places. Come on down. It's peaceful here and there's room for two on this log."

"I thought you might be saving that for Deb. Didn't you see her?"

"Sure I did," Andy said. And then, with a grin that lightened up his face and set the birds to singing more brightly, he added, "And I made sure that she didn't see me. Come on. What're you waiting for?"

Caro hesitated, then with a little shrug, stepped down the slope to the wooden shrine. She added the rose that Mr. Jiménez had given her to the glass of flowers on the shelf and then went and sat beside Andy.

They both started to speak at the same instant. Both stopped with a laugh. "You win," Andy said. "What were you going to say?"

"Nothing much," she answered. "Just that I had a nice walk. How about you?"

"Not much. Did you see the old man?"

"Yes."

"Well?"

"I don't want to tell you what he said because I'm afraid you'll want us to show the letter to Matilde right away. But I will tell you if you remember that you promised to wait for a couple of days and—"

"Hey," he interrupted. "Did you know that you have a bunch of leaves in your hair and a dusty old spider web across the front of your shirt?"

"I do?" Quickly, she brushed her T-shirt.

"No spiders," he said as he picked a leaf from her head and handed it to her. "Leave the rest alone. I already know that you clean up nicely."

He grinned at her again and Caro thought, I hope the birds are singing loudly because otherwise he'll hear my dumb heart hammering away. What's going on? First, I want to comfort him and now what I want . . . She didn't finish her thought because Andy put his arm around her and inched closer to her. She started to say something to hide her feelings but quickly changed her mind. Instead she raised her face to Andy's and waited for his kiss.

Caro closed her eyes as their lips came together. The warm, soft sea breeze played with her hair. After a few seconds, she pushed away from him, sighed, and with a little grin said, "I've got to admit that was nice."

"Come on!" Andy said, shaking his head. "Nice. Is that all? I kind of thought more like stupendous. I've been wanting to do that since I first saw you. There you were in Greg's Market, looking so dragged out and miserable in front of Deb. You were acting so tough. If I hadn't been so sunk in my own misery, I would've come on to you right then."

"Dragged out and miserable," Caro said slowly. "Was there a compliment hidden in there somewhere?"

"What do you think?" Andy said and kissed her again.

Chapter 10

🦋 "That's what I figured," Andy said as they walked back to Las Mariposas. Caro had just finished telling him what she had learned from Mr. Jiménez. "So now we know that the letter was written to Matilde by her grandfather."

Caro shrugged. "Who knows? It might even have been meant for my mother, but I doubt it. That is, if it was my great grandfather who wrote it. We still aren't positive. What we need now is a sample of his handwriting."

"Right, Chief," Andy said with a mock sober look. And then he added, "That should be easy. Matilde must have some of his old papers around."

"But we don't want Tía Matilde in on this yet. Remember?"

"All right, then. I'll check with my mom. She's bound to have something. She saves everything."

"Good. And I'll poke around too."

They parted at the eucalyptus trees. Halfway across the little meadow, Caro turned to catch one more glimpse of Andy, but he was hidden by the trees. She waved, just in case he was looking, and turned back toward the house.

As she stepped through the kitchen door, she heard the front door slam loudly. "Tía Matilde?" she called, hurrying up the hall. "Matilde, are you all right?"

Matilde was leaning against the doorjamb of her room, her face pale, her eyes wide with emotion. "No!" she answered sharply. "I'm not all right. I'm mad as—mad as a hornet!" Then, with an attempt at a smile, she said, "Help me to my couch, please, Caro. I'm not too steady at the moment and my cane's somewhere out there by the front door."

As Caro walked Matilde to the couch, she saw through the front windows a sleek gray car backing out of the driveway. It curved sharply onto the roadway and shot forward in a burst of speed.

"Whoever made you mad drives a great car," Caro said. "A new Lexus. And he's in a hurry."

"The mayor," Matilde muttered.

"Oh. Oh, no. I'm sorry."

"Yes. More bad news. Sit down, Caro."

Caro sat on the floor beside the small couch, her knees hugged to her chest. "So what's wrong this time?"

"You."

"Me? What did I do?"

"Nothing. Except to be an angel and help me cook our breakfasts. But the mayor's determined to force me to sell this house. And he's going to do it by making Las Mariposas fail as a B&B. So what he's up to now is to get the Health Department after me. He says that food handlers in this county have to have a clearance for tuberculosis. I've never heard of such a thing. Anyway, when I asked you—or Luisa—to come and help, I didn't expect you to handle food. I didn't expect to break my foot either. Or to have the Browns show up unexpectedly and . . . oh, what's the use? If he's right, there'll be a citation and the kitchen will be closed and . . ." She sighed. "He's going to beat me yet."

"No, he's not!"

Matilde shook her head slowly. "I know how you feel, honey, and I appreciate it, but that man's not giving up."

"Neither should you," Caro said firmly. "Besides, I think he's wrong. Guess what I did in July? I worked in a day camp where part of my job was to fix snacks to give little kids twice a day. Guess again. I had to have a TB clearance before I got that job, but it had nothing to do with the food. It had to do with being around little kids. But if what the mayor wants is someone with a TB clearance in your kitchen, he's got it. Even if it isn't required. If we call my mom right now, all she has to do is walk over to the center, borrow my records, and fax them to you. You could have them before supper."

Matilde's stiff shoulders relaxed. She smiled and said, "You never cease to surprise me, Caro. You can drive an old truck with a stick shift. You can make cholesterol-free crepes, and now, again, you turn up with just what I need to calm me down: common sense." A little grin came and went on her face as she added, "and a TB clearance to boot."

Caro asked, "Why do you suppose he didn't call the Health Department to get his facts straight before he tried to scare you again?"

A dark, thoughtful look covered Matilde's face as she said, "Jerome does stupid things when he gets panicky, and we've thwarted him more than he ever expected. Well, let's hope that he's already figured out what a dumb move this was. But, just in case, go call your mother."

By supper time, everything that was expected to arrive had arrived. Caro's employment record, including the results of the TB test, announced itself on the fax machine in Matilde's office just after the two would-be geologists, were settled in the Meadow Room. The two women were down again almost immediately, looking to greet Cloud and Pancake before they left in search of an antique shop and a restaurant that Matilde had recommended.

Two other arrivals, not necessarily planned but nonetheless expected, were Andy and Sara. They came while Caro and Matilde were seated at the kitchen table, finishing their supper, an omelet topped with leftover ratatouille.

When Andy asked, "What's new?" Matilde said, "Jerome's been at it again." She went on to tell them of the mayor's visit and how Caro and she had resolved it.

Caro said, "We figured he was in panic mode, not thinking too clearly."

"Brad called it his moron methodology," Andy said. "Sorry, Miss Matilde."

Matilde nodded and said, "I know. It really hurt Brad when his father acted that way."

"Do you have a will, Miss Matilde?" Andy asked. "A legal one. Done by a lawyer and all that?"

"Yes," Matilde said. "And Jerome knows what's in it. The house is really all I have and it will go to my sister, Caro's mother, when I die. No, Andy, I don't think he will do me physical harm." She smiled and looked fondly from one to the other of the three. "I've never felt so well cared for in all my life." And then, as Sara started to pick up their dishes and carry them to the sink, she said, "Stop that now. I've had a long rest. I'll do that. You three go do something young. Don't worry about me so much."

Sara said, "Are you sure, Miss Matilde? Oh, not about the worrying, about the dishes. I'll be glad to do them."

"I'm sure about both," Matilde said firmly. "Now do as I say, go, all of you. And, for heaven's sake, take the rest of those cookies with you."

Caro shot her aunt a glance. She had sounded just like her own mother. Maybe Matilde did have some of her sister's spunk. You go, girl, Caro thought with a grin, and that's the way to talk to the mayor too. "Sure," she said,

"I'll go, but they're my supper dishes too. I'll just put them in the dishwasher."

They left Matilde at the computer in her office and sat under the elm in the back garden. It was sunset and the colors that had filled the western sky were slowly melting from a fiery red to a blush of apricot as the sun dropped beyond the horizon.

Sara said, "Oh, the sky's so beautiful," and, as if in accord, they watched the sun set silently.

Caro was surprised to find out how tired she was. After all, she thought, I've done nothing today but wash my clothes and walk down the hill to see Mr. Jiménez. Maybe the tiredness is all the worrying about Matilde. Or taking on so much responsibility. Maybe my father is right. No way! She straightened up in her chair and glanced at Andy. She thought of the kisses they had shared and, suddenly, she wasn't tired anymore. It wasn't as if she hadn't been kissed before. There had been other boyfriends: the box boy at Lozano's, and then there was Max, and those movie dates where he never wanted to watch the movie. Of course, there was Ernie. Although it didn't take long for both of them to decide that they would rather be kissing someone else. Even so, Ernie and she had remained real friends. But there had been something different about kissing Andy. It was as if she had found something that, without knowing it, she had been looking for.

Andy grinned at her. "Hey, Chief," he said, "don't you want a report?"

"Yes," Sara said, "we brought a note Don Armando wrote to Mamá and Papá on an anniversary. I think it's the same writing as on that letter you found."

"So do I," Andy added, "but we'd better check anyway."

Caro jumped up. "I'll go get the letter."

Ten minutes later the two letters had been compared, and they concluded that they had both been written by Don Armando.

"What do we do now?" Sara asked eagerly.

"Find the other half of the letter," Caro said with a sigh.

"Could be on the other side of the world," Andy said.

"Could be," Caro answered reluctantly. And then, sitting up abruptly, she said, "But no. Whatever Don Armando left for her, he must have left around here. He knew that Matilde wasn't too tough, more of a . . . a homebody, you know, not adventurous."

"Like your mom?" Andy said.

"Absolutely. Los Angeles may not be that far away, but my mom would have gone to . . . to Upper Mongolia to be with my father. But Matilde is the stay-at-home type and Don Armando wouldn't have left stuff for her that she'd have to go to New York for. So, if the stuff's here, I'll bet the other half of the letter is around here somewhere." She took a deep breath and added, "We could brainstorm, you know, just throwing out places and ideas as to where it might be or what might have happened to it until someone pops up with an idea that makes sense. Maybe you guys will think that's a crazy move, but it works, really it does."

"Actually, it's a good idea," Andy said. And then, with an apologetic smile, he added, "But I've got to go. I'm driving Mrs. Shaw to Oak Valley to pick up her grandkids. I'll probably be a while."

"Sure," Caro said, hiding her disappointment. "Sara and I will come up with something."

After Andy left, Sara and Caro tossed ideas back and forth for a while and then agreed to sleep on it and try again the next day. Sara left, calling out a cheerful goodbye, and Caro stayed under the elm.

It was cool in the garden and pleasant once more to be alone. Well, not entirely alone. An enthusiastic chorus of crickets shared the yard with her. Darkness fell. When the moon slipped through a rolling bank of fog, the garden seemed filled with new shapes and shadows. In its light the rose bushes that were entwined on the rail fence threw lacelike patterns on the grass. A slight scent of jasmine reached her and she twisted in her chair, scanning the yard, wondering where the jasmine vine might be. In a moment she sat back, but almost immediately stiffened and leaned forward again. She had seen a movement near the shrubs by the back door. One of the cats, she thought until she realized that the movement was not in the shrubs. One side of the divided cellar door was moving slowly, as if being pushed from the inside. Not the cats, no, they couldn't do that.

Caro rose quickly. She would be in the direct line of sight of anyone leaving the cellar. She needed to hide, and her best bet would be the shrubs near the house. Silently, she moved away from her chair, making a wide arc toward the house. Her heart raced as she slid between two shrubs; the cellar door was still moving. For an instant she thought that it might be Mr. Ruiz; he had been here in the back yard during the late afternoon. That calming thought dissolved almost before it was completed because good sense told her that if Mr. Ruiz had business in the cellar, he wouldn't have closed the doors above him. Whoever was in the cellar was sneaking out cautiously in the yard. No, it was not Mr. Ruiz. Whoever it was was an intruder.

Caro held her breath as the person in the cellar lowered the half door slowly to one side of the opening. The hinges made a rough, rasping sound. Even through her fear, Caro thought of her father. No hinges or anything else in their house ever squeaked; her father was a fanatic with an oil can. In Matilde's cellar, the intruder froze at the raspy sound but, in an instant, began to move again, looking around carefully at each step upward. Cautiously, Caro peered around the edge of the shrub. It was a man in the cellar. No. No, it was a boy, a boy wearing a red-and-white kerchief tied pirate-wise around his head. But who? At that moment the moon was swallowed up by the high fog, leaving the garden in darkness once more. As if on cue, the crickets' chorus grew louder. A shadow detached itself from the cellar door, flipped on a small flashlight and, moving now with more purpose, headed on the walkway right toward her.

Caro stiffened. She never knew when the decision was made, or if a decision had been made, but when the boy came close, she steadied her stance, knees slightly bent, arms raised, and, with a loud "Hi-ya!," sprang at the boy. His flashlight flew into the rose-filled rail fence with a soft tinkle of broken glass, his breath exploded in a startled gasp and he landed on his back on the grass. She was about to lunge at him, reverting from karate to street fighting, when the boy whimpered, "Don't hurt me, please, don't hurt me!"

Caro remained at a safe distance. "All right," she said, "so long as you don't pull any sudden moves." The boy sat up slowly. Caro asked, "Are you okay? Who are you, anyway?"

There was no need for an answer. At that moment the moon reappeared and its light fell on a mass of red curls that had escaped the pirate's kerchief.

"Holy cheese!" Caro said. "Deb, what the heck are you doing here?"

Chapter 11

🦋 "You!" Deb snarled. "How dare you attack me!"

"Easy," Caro answered quickly. "You came sneaking out of the cellar like a bandit and made a bee-line for me. When someone comes at me that way, I don't stop to ask questions."

"A beeline for you? I didn't even know you were there."

"Sure. And I was supposed to know that?"

Deb pushed herself up off the ground, brushed herself off and said, "What were you going to do if you hadn't recognized me? Beat me up?"

"Sure. Probably. You sounded like an easy mark."

"Is that so?" Deb said with a toss of her red curls. "You might've been surprised."

They glared at each other for a long moment and then, as if on cue, they both burst out laughing.

"I don't know what's so funny," Deb said, the whine returning to her voice. "I've been cooped up in that moldy cellar for hours and I'm starving."

"What were you doing there? Did you get locked in?"

"Nobody locked me in. I just didn't want anyone to know I'd been in there. So I had to wait till everybody was gone." She pressed her lips into a thin line, shook her head and added, "Only you weren't gone."

"So what were you doing down there?"

Deb ignored her. "I'm going," she said. "I'm starving, remember?"

"Hold everything!" Caro cried. "You were breaking and entering. That's against the law. My aunt will want to know why."

"Don't tell Mattie," Deb said. "Please. Why would you want to do that?"

"Oh, come on now. It's obvious. What were you doing there?"

Deb drew in her breath and let it out slowly. "If I tell you, you can't tell Mattie. Promise."

"Holy cheese, Deb! *Promise?* How can I promise anything until I know what you're talking about?"

"I wasn't doing anything bad in the cellar. Honest. I was just looking for something."

"In the *cellar?* What?"

"I can't tell you that. I promised Brad." Deb's voice broke on the last syllable and started to cry.

Caro stared at her. Why did I ever think she was tough? "Hey," she said, "I just remembered. We have some great oatmeal cookies left over from lunch. Would you like some?"

Deb brushed a tear from her cheek. "Would I ever. Angela's oatmeal cookies. Where? Where are they?"

Six plump cookies were left on the paper plate under the elm, and it wasn't until Deb had devoured four of them that she spoke again. "Thanks. I guess I'll live." She leaned back in the chair. Finally, she said, "It was probably pretty stupid to go prowling around like that, but . . . You know what? I gotta get going." She jumped up and just as quickly sat down again. "Maybe I should talk to someone."

Caro clamped her mouth shut on the words that were ready to tumble out of her, "Sure. Go ahead. It'll do you good to talk." Deb wanted to say something, but it was clear that advice, well-intentioned or not, would turn her off.

"I . . . I promised Brad," she said finally. "He didn't want anyone else to know. He made me promise even though I didn't agree with him. I told him he should tell Mattie, but he said he couldn't. He said it was too . . . too personal, or close, or something like that."

Caro wanted to say, "Personal? Close? What the heck does that have to do with your roaming around in the cellar?" Instead, she held out the plate with the remaining two cookies. Deb took one and sat back, chewing slowly. Caro said, "Sounds like you *really* want to tell somebody. You're probably right. And maybe Tía Matilde is the one you should be talking to."

"I can't!" Deb cried. "Brad wouldn't want that!" She caught her breath and in a series of little sniffs and held-back sobs, Deb began to cry again.

Caro stared at her for a moment, then said, "I'll get you a Kleenex. And how about a glass of milk?"

Deb nodded between sobs.

In the house Caro grabbed a box of tissue in the laundry room, poured a glass of milk, and rushed outside.

Deb was gone.

Even with both sides of the cellar door pulled open and the early morning sun beginning to shine through the mist, the cellar was dark and shadowy.

Caro paused at the top of the steps that led into the basement room and ran her flashlight's beam along the walls and then on each step as she descended. She had gone to bed right after Deb left the night before, but had slept fitfully, eager for morning to come so that she could discover what had drawn Deb to the cellar. Now, as she stood in the center of the musty, cement-walled room, she had to wonder if getting up at dawn had been worth it. Except for a small pile of wooden boards four or five feet long and tied neatly with green nylon string in one corner and a couple of broken kitchen chairs in another, there was nothing in the cellar but an abundance of cobwebs that seemed to have captured several years' worth of dust along with an assortment of dead and drying insects. Showing above her head was the subflooring of the house and the pipes for plumbing. Well, Caro thought, Deb certainly wasn't looking for anything to be hidden in this place; there isn't a corner that isn't exposed. So what had she been doing down here and what had she promised Brad not to spill? And why especially not to Matilde? The cellar was part of her house, after all.

With a shrug Caro turned toward the steps, but as she did she caught sight of some powdery stuff on the floor in the corner by the broken chairs. Above it she could see that someone had been poking and scraping in and around one of the old cracks that patterned the cement walls. Another careful look with the flashlight showed that someone—Deb, for sure—had dug into several other cracks, each time leaving a sandy residue of dry cement on the floor. Caro flipped off the flashlight and started up the steps. So Deb hadn't been lying. She had been looking for something. Caro pulled the cellar doors closed and paused to look around her. The morning sun already was sending dappled shafts of sunlight through the elm tree. It was going to be a beautiful day.

Back in the house Caro just had time to make coffee and set the small table in the kitchen before the two would-be geologists appeared, ready for breakfast.

Matilde was right behind them. "Sorry, Caro," she said in a whispered aside, "I moved very slowly this morning." To the two ladies she said, "Oatmeal or Cream of Wheat? And how would you like your eggs?"

By midmorning the chores were done. The two industrious and thoughtful guests had made their own beds and left a note saying they had no need yet for clean sheets or towels. Hooray! And the kitchen, with Matilde's insistent help, took Caro only a few minutes to clean. Then Matilde and she talked about the breakfasts for Friday, Saturday, and Sunday. They agreed to repeat the menus they had used the previous weekend.

"Except," Matilde said, "we're running out of Angela's frozen coffee cakes and muffins, so, tomorrow on your shopping trip to Oak Valley, will you stop at the bakery? Can you believe it's called, 'The Sugar and Spice'?"

"Sure, I'll believe it," Caro said, "so long as it smells that way. Is it near Al's Market?"

"One block away," Matilde said. "Take it easy today, Caro. Starting tomorrow we'll be pretty busy. Lots of guests."

"We'll manage," Caro said, nodding somberly, and realized that she had sounded just like her mother. "Okay, then," she added, "if you really don't need me, I'll go hang with Sara." *And* Andy she thought as she moved to the back door.

It was Andy that she saw first. He was at the side of the white clapboard house helping Mr. Ruiz load gardening equipment into the back of an aging pickup truck. Beside them, Tony was busy rolling up a garden hose. He looked up, saw Caro, and waved.

Andy turned. "'Morning, Chief," he called over his shoulder. "Sara and I were coming over as soon as I finished here."

"Too late. I got here first. Hello, Mr. Ruiz. Hi, Tony."

"Good morning, Carolina." Mr. Ruiz picked up the hose that Tony had rolled up and swung it into the back of the pickup.

Mr. Ruiz and Tony got into the truck. They said good-bye and backed the pickup away from the house and on to a narrow road that cut into the walnut groves.

"Hey, Caro!" Sara called from the front porch of the house. "Is it time for the brainstorming?"

"Sure," Caro said, "but let me tell you about Deb first." Andy and she walked to the porch, where they all sat on the steps while she described what had gone on with Deb the night before. "This morning I went into the cellar," she ended, "and found that she'd been poking into the cracks in the walls. She was definitely looking for something."

"Something so small that it would fit in a crack," Andy said, "or something big that might be hidden behind a hinged panel in the wall. Gives us a lot of objects to choose from."

"Hm-m-m," Sara said softly. "That could take a long time to figure out. At least with the letter we know what we're looking for."

"Right," Caro said. "So I guess we shouldn't take time to track down what she was looking for. Not when we have our other problem to deal with."

"I'm glad you feel that way," Andy said. "Anyway, my guess is that whatever she's looking for is probably something Brad hid when we were kids. Suddenly, Deb thought about it and had to have it. She can be darned flaky at times."

Caro frowned. "I don't know. She was pretty torn up last night and pretty determined not to break her promise to Brad. What's more she was really shaken at the idea that Matilde might find out that she'd been snooping. No, whatever she was after, I don't think it was insignificant. It was like she was driven to find it. Imagine staying in that dark cellar for several hours just so no one would know what she was doing? Well, maybe she'd be suspicious of me, but why *you* guys? You all grew up together, didn't you?"

Sara nodded briskly. "But Deb's never been afraid of anything."

"Well, she *was* last night," Caro said. "I think she was really afraid of two things: that we'd find out what she was doing and that if I was too nice to her she might break her promise to Brad. You know, and tell me whatever she'd promised not to. Look at how she disappeared when I went in to get her some milk."

"Maybe you're right," Andy said. "But we're still right back where we started. Are we going to spend our time trying to figure out Deb or are we going to concentrate on Matilde's letter?"

"Matilde's letter!" Sara and Caro said simultaneously.

"Tía Matilde's letter, of course," Caro added firmly. Then her face puckered into a frown. "Unless . . . unless . . . unless there's a connection." She closed her eyes and said, "Something's playing hide-and-seek in my brain, something that says— There! I know. It's . . . it's . . . Oh, shoot, it's gone again."

"Just forget about it," Andy said. "It'll come to you later. Meanwhile, while we're waiting for inspiration on our next move, let's take a look at the cellar. Maybe we can cross it off our list of mysteries."

Chapter 12

🦋 The inspection of the cellar had to be postponed. A phone call for Caro at María's house brought them all back to Las Mariposas in a hurry.

"Thank you, thank you, thank you," Matilde said as she met them at the back door. "All three of you came. There are two unexpected guests in the parlor. I told them I'd have to discuss it with my helpers. They're here to participate in the Oak Valley Fair, but there was a mix-up with their hotel reservations and Al, from Al's Market, sent them here." She took a deep breath. "What do you think? Can we house them and feed them for two nights? Their hotel has them scheduled starting Thursday."

Caro had the refrigerator door open. "One-and-a-half dozen eggs left. There's bacon and a little ham. There's fruit too. Cantaloupe and some strawberries and lots of cranberry and orange juice."

Sara called from the freezer. "There are three kinds of muffins and one coffee cake in here."

"That should do it, shouldn't it?" Caro said. "So, now it's up to you. Are you up to it?"

"Yes, I think so," Matilde replied.

"I'll help," Sara said.

"I'll go get their luggage," Andy said. "What room does it go in?"

"The Ocean Room," Matilde answered. "That room is not reserved until Friday."

Leslie and Ron Kurtner, the unexpected guests, were exultant and effusive in their appreciation. They loved the Ocean Room and insisted that a very simple breakfast would do. Then, almost as suddenly as they had come, they left for Oak Valley.

Matilde disappeared into her office after thanking her three helpers again.

Andy's cell phone jingled and he headed out to the backyard to take his call.

Sara edged over to the back door. "Come on, Caro," she said, "I can't wait. Let's go look in the cellar."

Outside, they found Andy already pulling open the cellar doors. "I've got a fare. Let's take a quick look before I go."

Caro handed Andy the flashlight she had brought with her. "Here. Take a look by yourself. We'll be right behind you."

Andy ran the beam of light around the cement-walled room while Sara and Caro waited halfway down the steps. "Hey," he said, "there's a light bulb up there. See? Hanging from that beam. The pull string's broken, but hold on, I think I can reach it."

The light from the dingy bulb served only to illuminate the cobwebs surrounding it; the corners of the room remained in darkness until the flashlight's beam reached them.

"It's just like you said, Chief," Andy said and threw her a smile. "Nothing here except evidence that someone's been poking into the cracks." He handed her the flashlight. "I'll turn that wimpy light off. Sorry I've got to run again. You guys start brainstorming without me."

Sara, who had been fumbling around with the broken chairs, looked up and said, "'Bye, Andy." And then,

"These look as if they could be fixed pretty easily. They match the two in the kitchen. And look at all those nice boards over there."

"And the nice cobweb I just walked into," Caro said.

They stayed in the cellar, each intent on what she was doing, Caro examining the walls, Sara fitting the pieces of the chairs together, until a shadow dimmed the light that came from the doorway.

"Hi! What'cha doing down there?"

With a loud gasp Sara dropped the broken chair legs she was holding. Caro spun around. Tony Jiménez, a wood-handled hoe in his hands, stood at the opening to the cellar.

"Oh, Tony," Sara moaned, "you scared the life out of me."

"I only asked what you were doing," Tony said and scuttled down the steps. "Nothing much down here, is there?"

"Nothing much," Caro answered and added, "What are you doing here, anyway? I thought you'd gone with Mr. Ruiz."

"We're back. I'm supposed to weed the whole side yard. I guess I'd better get going." He didn't move. His eyes circled the room and paused at the neatly tied wooden boards. A grin filled his face as he shook his head and said, "So that's where he left them. Wait'll I tell Uncle Pete."

"The chairs?" Sara asked.

"Nah. The boards. He swore there was a pile of four-inch boards, all four-feet long and tied with green nylon twine in our cellar, some boards he'd put there several years ago. When he couldn't find them, he lost it. He went ballistic. Swore somebody'd stolen them." Tony shrugged.

THE TRUTH ABOUT LAS MARIPOSAS   101

"Well, he finally calmed down and actually bought some more lumber for the shed he was building."

"And you think those are the ones he was looking for?" Caro asked.

"Sure. They were leftovers from a job he'd done for Don Armando just before the old man died. I was a little kid then but I remember how Uncle Pete was always building things for him." Tony grinned again. "I guess I'd better not tell my uncle where the boards are. Might make him feel bad."

"Good thinking," Caro said. "Okay, Tony, lead the way. We're ready to go now. If there's anything of interest down here, we didn't find it."

Sara and Caro were in Caro's bedroom giving the old desk another going over when Andy returned. He thrust his head in the open doorway and said, "Hungry?"

"Oh, my gosh," Sara cried, sniffing, "I smell pizza. Tell me I do, Andy, tell me I do!"

"What else?" Andy said. "Compliments of Miss Matilde who buzzed me on my cell phone and placed the order. They're all pepperoni and . . ."

"And mushrooms, I hope," Caro said.

"And mushrooms," Andy replied.

The kitchen smelled warm and spicy. Matilde was on her stool, the open pizza boxes on the counter before her. She was slicing them into wedges. "Here," she said, "take them into the back garden. Have a picnic. I'll have mine right here and then get back to work."

"Cokes?" Caro asked.

"Cokes, of course," Matilde answered her. "We have a truckload of them."

Outside, they spread their picnic on the table under the elm and, with Tony joining them, three large pepperoni pizzas disappeared in a matter of minutes. When they had finished, including chasing down crumbs and straggling cheese strings, they cleaned up the mess and Tony went off to pull weeds in the side yard.

"So?" Andy said. "How'd the brainstorming go?"

"Not far," Sara said with a giggle. "We searched the cellar and then the desk again."

"I've been thinking," Caro said. "A lot of things seem to be happening around here. Maybe instead of just concentrating on where the letter might be, maybe we should make a list . . ." She paused when she saw Andy's skeptical expression, but then nodded firmly and said, "Yes. A written list so we can see if any of the incidents have a connection with each other. Okay, okay. Yes, that funny feeling that there *is* a connection is still bumping around in my mind. Maybe it's about the mayor's wanting to get Matilde to sell the house and about Deb's searching the cellar. Maybe it's about Brad's dying and the letter in the old desk. Or maybe it's about Brad's borrowing Matilde's car and . . . and . . . oh, well, the dumb broken chairs in the cellar."

"Or the pile of boards," Sara said giggling again. "I'm just kidding. But, anyway, I think it's a great idea. Let's do it."

Andy added, "All right. I guess it's better than sitting here empty-headed just looking at each other."

"Speak for yourself, Andy," Caro said. "I've got at least one thing bumping around in my otherwise empty head."

"Sorry, Chief," Andy said with a grin, "no insult intended."

Caro went inside the house and brought out paper and pencils. She said, "Let's write down anything and everything weird that's happened in—what do you guys think?—the last three months?"

"Particularly the last three months," Andy said, "but it should be everything weird that's happened any time if it's associated with Las Mariposas or Miss Matilde. Only . . ." He paused and shook his head. "You're not going to like this, Chief. I still can't see how this is going to help us trace that letter."

"I can't either," Caro said with a shrug, "but maybe it'll help the mess in my mind."

Andy looked at her, a thoughtful frown on his face. "You really had an insight, didn't you?"

"Yes, but it came and went so fast that I haven't a clue as to what it was about."

"Okay," Andy said. "Let's get started on our lists."

It took a lot of mumbled, "Ohs" and "Ahs" and "Hm-m-ms" and a sigh or two from Sara, but, in less than twenty minutes, the lists were done. They merged them into one, arranging them in order of importance to Matilde and her life. Number one was the mayor's con-niving to get Matilde out of the house, followed unanimously by the letter in the old desk.

"That letter, if we ever find out what it's all about, might really change Tía Matilde's life," Caro said.

"But what does it have to do with the mayor?" Sara asked. "It's like they should be on separate lists."

"No," Andy answered her. "Remember, we're listing everything unusual that's been happening around Miss Matilde."

"Well, how about her broken foot?" Sara shot back. "Nobody put *that* down."

Caro nodded and said, "That's right. That really changed a lot of things for her. Do you suppose . . . no, let's just put it down."

The combined list grew with Brad's dying mentioned solemnly by all. Of course, Deb's strange behavior in the cellar came next.

They were quiet for a little while and then Sara said, "Oh. Your coming here was unusual, too, Caro. Maybe we should . . ."

"Put me down," Caro interrupted. "Who knows? Maybe my being here does fit in somewhere."

"Sure it does," Andy said with a smile and she felt a little shiver of pleasure. Then he added, "Speaking of where you fit in, I have a thought."

"Out of your empty head?" Sara asked. "Are you sure?"

Andy feigned a punch at her chin and said, "Watch yourself, little sister. Yes, I'm sure. Look, Caro, there must be some of Don Armando's papers around. Couldn't you tell Matilde that you're terribly interested in your ancestry and ask if you can see them? Maybe there'd be something in them that would give us a clue as to what was in the first page of that letter."

"Great idea," Caro said. "And I'd better ask her today, because starting tomorrow and through next week things will be hopping around here."

"It's because of the fair," Sara said. "But after tomorrow — because tomorrow I'm working with my mother — we'll all be helping Miss Matilde. And most of the guests, especially if they're part of the Oak Valley Fair, will be gone after breakfast."

"Let's hope," Caro said. "What kind of a fair is it? Like a county fair, with millions of booths and cows and hens and home-made jams?"

Andy laughed. "No cows. Mostly it's artsy-craftsy, with displays of pottery and weaving, you know, that kind of stuff. There'll be the work of some really good painters too. Of course, there'll be homemade pies and cakes and jams and jellies, all fighting for ribbons. The best part though is the big Ferris wheel . . ."

"And the merry-go-round," Sara interrupted.

"And hot dog stands?" Caro asked.

"Sure," Andy replied. "Tell you what. I'll go with you to pick up the groceries tomorrow, but first we'll get some hot dogs at the fair."

"I'd like that," Caro said, getting up, "so long as they come with chopped onions."

Andy grimaced. "It takes all kinds," he said. "Meanwhile, go see what you can learn about your ancestors."

Chapter 13

🦋 Matilde looked at Caro with surprise.

"It's funny you should ask," she said. "I just ran into a copy of my grandfather's will in my little safe and I realized how few papers he had left behind when he died."

Caro said, "It's not important. I was just interested in knowing more about my ancestors. Like where Don Armando's parents came from and all that. My mother doesn't seem to know anything at all."

Matilde, who was lying on the little couch near the windows of her room, pushed up into a sitting position and said, "Neither do I. My grandparents said very little about their past. Once, when your mother put her foot down and demanded answers to her questions, Papacito became very angry and said, '*¡Basta!* You are not to question me again! We are here now. This is *our* country. We will forget about our past.' I don't know about your mother, but *I* never had the courage to ask any more questions."

"Mr. Jiménez says they came here escaping from a revolution or something. Is that true?"

"It was more like 'or something.' But I don't know exactly what. That's when our parents were killed and our grandparents brought us here. We lived a very quiet life, especially after your mother left. Papacito was not easy to live with and Mamacita rarely raised her voice. You can guess how much I missed your mother. She was the laughter in my life. Then Mamacita died and, soon after,

Papacito, and I was left alone. Your mother insisted that I come to live with your family, but I loved this old house and I had friends here, so I stayed. And then because I was lonely and he was charming . . he can be charming, you know . . ." Matilde paused and shrugged, ". . . I married Jerome."

"The mayor?"

Matilde nodded. "And then my quiet life ended," she said with a rueful smile. "But there was Brad."

"I'm sorry, Tía. I didn't mean to bring up sad things."

"You didn't. They were with me before you came in. But back to what you were asking. The only papers Papacito left are things like receipts and business letters from the last years of his life. They're not very important. I saved them in an old shoe box. I don't know why. But you're certainly welcome to look through them if you want."

"Thank you," Caro said in a small voice because, suddenly, she was uncomfortable at not being completely honest with her aunt. Maybe Andy was right. Maybe Matilde should be told *right now* about the letter from the old desk. But when she glanced back at Matilde from the doorway, she shook her head. No. Her aunt had enough unhappy stuff going on as it was. The incomplete letter would only add more. One more day—or two—surely shouldn't matter. And who knows? Maybe they'd know more about the letter by then. She bit her lip. Maybe.

After supper Caro took the shoe box with Don Armando's papers into her room. She found that there was nothing in the box of any interest: only three or four letters from a bank and a couple from a fire insurance agency. The rest were paid bills and receipts. Not only were they boring, but they were pretty useless. She sighed and flipped on the television. For a while a rerun of "Seinfeld" kept her attention and then she returned to the box. More receipts. Several from the Oak Valley Artists' Supply and a few from a lumber yard, one for pine boards cut in four-foot lengths. She thought of the leftover wood in the cellar and wondered what Mr. Jiménez had built for Don Armando.

After the Kurtners left the next morning Caro returned the box to Matilde. "You were right," she said. "There's nothing here. I'll put it in your office, okay?" When she came back to the kitchen where Matilde was having a cup of coffee, she said, "Andy offered to show me around the fair when I go for our groceries today. Is that okay or do you want me back right away? I'll do both the Kurtners' room and the kitchen before I go. I'm getting good at it, you know."

"And I'm getting good at moving around. So take your time at the fair."

Andy and Caro arrived at Oak Valley Park at noon, just in time for the ribbon-cutting ceremony that marked the opening of the fair. It was hot so they watched the proceedings standing in the spotty shade of a scrawny tree at a distance from the waiting crowd. A group of fair officials and a paunchy, balding middle-aged man stood beside a wide ribbon that was stretched between two tall sycamore trees. Behind them a trio of guitarists wearing flowered cotton shirts over khaki shorts strummed their guitars lazily as they waited. After some hurried discussion among the officials, there was a long pulsing chord from the guitarists, and the formalities began. The fair queen was presented and then the paunchy man, introduced as the mayor of Oak Valley, said a few words and officially opened the fair by cutting the broad ribbon with a pair of immense scissors.

A round of applause and some cheering followed, and then the crowd moved forward into a field of colorful tents and booths, flanked here and there by bright umbrella tables. A Ferris wheel, standing high in the background, began moving and, at the same time, the notes of a calliope, the music of the merry-go-round, filtered through the air.

"All right," Caro said, "*where* is the hot dog stand?"

"I'd say let's follow the crowd," Andy answered, "and we're bound to find it. It's lunch time, remember?"

They found the hot dogs, but not before they found a booth selling tacos whose hot, spicy scent made them almost irresistible to Caro. Andy grabbed Caro's arm and hurried her by a long table spread with trays of fudge and rich cookies. "Over there," he said, "hot dogs, at last."

They sat at an umbrella table with their hot dogs and icy drinks. When they were done, they decided that they had time enough to wander around a bit. They watched a potter turning a small pot under a canvas canopy while a smiling young woman attended to the beautiful pots and bowls that were for sale. They passed tables displaying jewelry, hand-painted silk scarves, and woven baskets of all shapes and sizes. There was a florist's booth that overflowed, not only with sprays of color, but also with the fresh fragrance of the flowers.

Caro paused by a potted plant of miniature yellow roses. "You know what?" she said with a little laugh. "I'm going to buy this for Tía Matilde. I guess I'm feeling guilty. Anyway, we ought to pick up the groceries and get on back. She told me not to hurry, but . . ."

"Not before we've had one ride," Andy said. "Sorry. No thrill rides at this fair, except for the merry-go-round. It's so old and rusty that just to make one full turn is a thrill. Come on." He took her arm and they started for the end of the fair grounds.

The brassy notes of "In the Good Old Summertime," came through clearly as they neared the merry-go-round. Abruptly, Andy stopped beside a tent-like canopy that covered a display of glass bottles and bowls. "Look, Caro," he said, indicating a small wooden booth decorated with signs of the zodiac and floating silk scarves, "that's Deb over there by the fortune teller's place. And what the heck's she doing?"

"I'd say snooping. She seems to be focusing on that man." As Caro spoke Deb darted from behind the garish booth to the protection of a tent that was filled with a jumble of Mexican objects: hanging piñatas, sarapes, baskets and immense hats. There Deb pushed herself into the jumble and, holding up a grass hat as cover, she watched the progress of a tall sandy-haired man wearing a white polo shirt.

"Well, I'll be darned," Andy said, "that's Mayor Poole she's tailing."

"The mayor?" Caro said. "Really?" The man in the polo shirt turned as he stopped to talk to a woman seated on a wooden bench and Caro added, "He doesn't look at all like I expected. He looks a lot like Brad, doesn't he?" Andy shrugged and then, as both the mayor and Deb moved again, she said, "Come on, let's go, Andy, let's see what's up."

When the mayor paused for a few minutes at a model train display and then made for the parking lot, Deb stopped following him. She came out onto the walkway and hurried to a booth labeled, "Coffee Express." She bought a tall latte topped with whipped cream and sat on a shaded bench to drink it.

"What do you suppose this is all about?" Caro said. "Should we ask her?"

"Later, Chief," Andy said. "You said we were short on time and you want a ride on the carousel, don't you?"

"I do? Okay, okay, I'd like a ride on the carousel."

An hour later, with the shaky merry-go-round ride over and Andy's SUV packed with Matilde's groceries, Andy and Caro were on their way back to Two Sands. She was having trouble putting the strains of the carousel's music out of her head. The tinny melodies kept pushing into and interrupting her thoughts about Deb. The more she dwelt on Deb's actions, the more certain she was that there was a clue there to all that had been happening—if she could only hold on to it long enough to recognize it. But she couldn't. It escaped her just as it had done yesterday morning as they sat on the Ruiz's porch. Still this almost awareness was a bit more solid. She could see some links. First, Brad had told Deb something that had to be kept secret and that seemed to be very important. Next, Deb had dug around in the cellar of Las Mariposas secretly. Underlying it all, the mayor wanted Matilde out of Las Mariposas and was pulling strings to persuade her. And now, Deb was tailing the mayor. "Yes!" she said. "There's a connection there!"

"Where? What? What are you talking about?" Andy asked, and she realized that she had spoken out loud.

"Guess I'm losing it," she said. "I didn't mean to burst out like that. I was trying to figure out what Deb was doing and I thought I'd found the connection to all that's been happening at Las Mariposas, but, if I did . . . No! When I did, it disappeared just as quickly as it came."

Andy's brow went up and he threw her a glance but said nothing.

They were turning off the highway on to Pier Road when she said, "Andy, how long have you known Deb?"

"Forever," he said, "or, at least, from the day I came to live with María and Juan, whichever came first. In other words," he added with a grin, "a long, long time. I was going on four, so she must've been two."

"Did she live close by or what?"

"Actually, she did and does, but María took care of Deb in our house every day, kind of like a nanny. So there I was, a mature four-year-old, stuck with a couple of two-year-old shadows. Let me tell you, it was a happy day for me when I went off to kindergarten."

Caro gave him a little smile and said, "What does her mother do? I mean, does she work somewhere?"

"Not that I know of," Andy said dryly. "She just plays golf and bridge and whatever else goes on in the Oak Valley Country Club. Deb's been pretty much on her own since she was eleven or twelve. Except for Mrs. Bayless, their housekeeper, that is."

"A housekeeper?" Caro said. "Wow."

"Yeah. They live in one of those big houses we passed on Pier Road. The one with the bright blue shutters."

"Oh, right. And two skinny palms. I remember. What's with her father?"

"Who knows? All I know is that there is no Mr. Ewing. Just Deb and her mom."

"Kind of a poor little rich girl, huh?"

"Not Deb. She's smart as a whip and as independent. She'll be all right." He smiled and shook his head slowly as he added, "Sara's gutsy too, but in a different way. She's not quite as nervy as Deb."

Caro looked at him and said, "You sound like a big brother, a little bit critical, a little bit proud."

"I guess I am."

"Hm-m-m." She felt uncomfortable, but still she felt compelled to ask, "I thought you said Deb was always coming on to you guys, you and Brad."

"Oh, that. You saw her. She still does it. With me it's just for practice, but I've come to believe it was for real with Brad."

"I think so too," Caro said.

They had arrived at Las Mariposas. Andy swung into the driveway, switched off the engine and turned to her. "What makes you say that?" he asked.

"It was the other night. She was all broken up. Not just about her promise to Brad. It was more than that. She . . . she was really suffering and she showed it. I guess I had scared the stuff out of her and she was too shaky and too hungry to remember to pull on a shell." Caro frowned, picking out her words carefully. "My mother says that people who are in emotional pain usually build tough shells around themselves, you know, to shield from being hurt even more. I didn't used to believe her, but I'm sure starting to. I think that Don Armando really hurt my mother, so she knew what she was talking about. And Deb. Look at what her mother must've done to her, ignoring her like that. Her father, too, for all we know. I'll bet the day I met Deb at Greg's Market that what she wanted most was to be sitting in a corner crying about losing Brad. But she didn't dare let herself go. Instead, there she was, cold and sharp and suffering inside her glossy little shell."

Andy was silent for a moment, a frown growing on his face. Finally, he said, "I guess you're right. She's always been . . . well, reserved . . . even as a little kid. She rarely cried. There were times when María would chew the three of us out for something really bad that we had done—like when we put painted rocks in the fishbowl and all our goldfish died—and Sara and I would end up bawling, but not Deb. She would just stare at María, clench her fists and stay dry-eyed. Yeah, you're right about the shell. I think she's always had it. I guess I was just too close to her to see it." He slapped the seat divider firmly and added, "Of course! Brad knew his feelings and Deb's were for real, but he didn't want to show them either so he, no, not just he, we made a game out of Deb's interest in him. I'm such a lamebrain! How dumb can I be?"

"Hey," Caro said quickly. "I caught Deb without her shell by accident. Besides, you were too close to both of them to see it. Come on, let's get the groceries out of the sun and into the house."

Chapter 14

🦋 After supper on that same day, Caro walked down Pier Road toward the house with the blue shutters.

She had told Matilde that she was going to see Deb, that they had seen her at the fair but had not had a chance to talk with her. That was all she had said. Nothing about the mayor and Deb's suspicious actions. It had surprised Caro to discover that lying by omission was as guilt-producing as telling a direct lie. The yellow roses had pleased Matilde, but they had done nothing to calm Caro's growing feelings of self-doubt and guilt.

She was so deep into her thoughts that she almost passed the house. It was the sudden appearance of two skinny palms marking the entrance to a driveway that stopped her. Round, pebbled stepping stones in a well-cut lawn led the way to three shallow steps, a small stoop and a front door that, like the shutters, was painted a bright blue. She rang the doorbell.

The door was opened by a tall slim woman whose gray dress almost exactly matched her clipped gray hair. Her face, except for a light flesh tone, was colorless. "Yes?" she said.

"Are you Deb's mom?" Caro asked. "Is Deb at home?"

"No and no. I'm Mrs. Bayliss, the housekeeper. Deb is rarely at home. You'll have to get her cell phone number when you next see her. That's the best way to catch her."

"Thanks," Caro said. "I'll do that." She swung around and as she did, she heard the sound of squealing tires.

"There she is," Mrs. Bayliss said and closed the door.

A shiny red sports car came to a stop on the driveway by the house. Deb jumped out of the car, slammed the car door and hurried toward the front steps. She stopped abruptly. "What're you doing here?" she asked.

"Looking for you," Caro said and sat down on the steps. "Can we talk?"

"What about?"

"I thought maybe you'd tell me what you know, if you know anything, about what's going on at Las Mariposas."

"But not about the other night," Deb said firmly. "I won't talk about that."

"Sure. Okay. Not that." Caro moved over on the cement stoop. Deb shrugged and sat down beside her. Caro said, "Okay if we talk about Brad? My aunt says he was really cool. That wasn't exactly the word she used, but that's what she meant."

"Yeah, he was cool," Deb said in a dull, flat tone. And then, with her voice rising, she said, "But Mattie says that about everybody. She's kind of a noodle. You know, a pushover. Like she married old man Poole, didn't she?"

"Maybe Tía Matilde's not very tough," Caro said, "but she's all right and she really loved Brad. She says that he was the only good thing that came from her marriage. And now, of course, he's gone." Caro bit her lip. She hadn't meant to say that.

"Yeah," Deb said with a harsh little laugh, "he's gone all right."

I should say I'm sorry, Caro thought, but, no, that would only make things worse. They were silent for a moment. Finally, she said, "Why were you following the mayor at the fair today?"

Deb stiffened. "Who said?" she snapped. "Who said?"

"I said," Caro answered. "Andy and I followed you as you tailed the mayor. And we stopped when you did. You know, when you bought that huge latte."

"You had no right to spy on me!"

"Oh, yes we did. For Pete's sake, Deb! Andy, Sara, and I are trying to help Tía Matilde because the mayor's trying to hurt her. I figure that you know something about Las Mariposas and about the mayor and I need you to tell me what it is. Please!"

"You said we weren't going to talk about the other night."

"Oh? I didn't even know that your following the mayor had anything to do with the other night, but maybe now I do. Please, Deb, what's going on?"

Deb hunched over her knees and shook her head. "You're nosy, you know? Anyway, I don't feel like talking."

"I've got to be nosy. I need to help my aunt." Caro stared straight ahead, her lips pressed into a thin line. Finally, she jumped up. "Thanks for nothing," she said and started across the stepping stones. Before she had reached the road, she took a few deep breaths, turned and said, "Well, if you won't tell me anything about the mayor or what you were doing in the cellar, maybe you'll answer this." Deb shook her head but Caro added quickly, "It's just about a letter Don Armando wrote Tía Matilde telling her about some stuff he'd left her, and I thought that just maybe . . . " Deb stood up and glared at her and Caro said, "Forget it, forget it. I don't know why I even asked you.

You can stop giving me dirty looks. It doesn't have anything to do with the other night."

"Really?" Deb said with a smirk. "How do you know?"

"Actually, I don't know that. Maybe it does."

"You don't know much, do you?"

"Right. I don't know much. And I have a feeling you don't know everything either." Caro straightened her shoulders. Deb knew something and she *had* to find out what it was. "Look," she said and walked back toward her, "maybe what I know and what you know put together might mean something important. That is, if we're after the same things. You know, like I want to help Tía Matilde and you, I guess, want to do something for Brad."

"I don't know anything about a letter," Deb said sulkily and sat down on the stoop again.

"All right, I give up. Forget the letter." She sat beside Deb once more. In the silence that followed she could almost hear her mother's voice whispering one of those wise sayings that annoyed Luisa and her so much because they were nearly always right: *If a wall stops your progress, don't climb over it until you look for a gate.*

Bueno, Mamá, Caro thought, where's the opening through this stubborn wall of Deb's? *Where?* She glanced at Deb's drained, hollow-eyed face and found the answer. Deb's one soft spot was Brad.

"I wish I'd known Brad," Caro said softly. "What was he like?"

Beside her Deb shrugged. "Just a regular guy."

Caro let out her breath and stared at the pale round moon that was showing in the twilight sky above the palms. What should she say now?. She turned, planning to ask more about Brad, but stopped when she saw tears streaming down Deb's cheeks.

"Oh, Deb," she said, "I'm sorry."

"Not half as much as I am. Besides, I shouldn't be crying; I don't even have a Kleenex."

"I do," Caro said and dug in her pocket. "They're rumpled but they're clean. Here, give me one back. You've got me crying too."

In a moment, out of the silence that had grown around them, came Deb's ragged voice. "I know why Brad died," she said. Caro drew in her breath. "He was trying to stop his father from hurting Mattie." She shook her head angrily. "*And it couldn't be done!* He wouldn't tell me the whole thing 'cause he said he didn't want me getting mixed up in it, but I know *that* much. And I know why he went to Oak Valley that night. He *had* to talk to someone. Maybe he did talk to him and maybe he didn't, but I know his basketball coach lived there and . . . and . . . and who cares? It doesn't matter anymore, anyway."

Caro swallowed hard. "Oh, Deb, I'm so sorry," she repeated.

"I know. I hate Mayor Poole. He had Brad so upset that half the time he didn't know what he was doing. It's his fault Brad got killed." Deb breathed deeply, a long breath broken by a stammering sob. "So when I heard the mayor tell a man in the antique pavilion that Las Mariposas would soon be his, I just *had* to follow him to see what else I could learn. A lot of good it did me. When he made a bee-line for the parking lot, I gave up."

"Yeah," Caro said dejectedly, "we already know he expects to get Las Mariposas. Why? What's there about it that makes him want it now? He already had it once, you know, when he was married to my aunt. He could've tried to get it when he divorced her, but no, he didn't seem to care then. Something must have happened since that time to change his mind."

Beside her, Deb blew her nose. "If anybody knows the answer to that," she said with a sniffle, "it's Brad. And . . . and he can't help us."

"Maybe he can," Caro said. "What did he tell you? What were you looking for in the cellar?"

Deb moaned. "There you go again. I told you I promised Brad not to tell."

"Not to tell what? You already told the most important part, that Brad was trying to save Tía Matilde *and* his father and that it was driving him crazy." She turned to face her. "Come on, Deb, help us. What else did he tell you?"

"Go away. Just leave me alone."

"I'm not going. Not yet, anyway. Not till I say this: You're trying to be loyal to Brad, but you aren't, really. I think Brad would want you to help Tía Matilde no matter what happens to the mayor. He wouldn't expect you to protect his father just because he was trying to. I can't believe you. You mean you're going to let Tía Matilde suffer just to protect the mayor?"

"You ask too many questions, you know?"

"I know." Caro stood up. "Okay, I'll leave. Just think about it, okay?"

"All right," Deb said. "I don't have to think about it. Besides, Brad didn't tell me that much. All he told me was that his father had taken something that belonged to Mattie and that when he, Brad, had a chance, he stole it away from him. So he could return it to Mattie, of course. And that while he figured out how best to do that, he'd hidden it in his favorite place, where it would be safe. But he didn't tell me where."

Caro's heart started to race. This had to be what Don Armando's letter was talking about. "What was it?" she asked eagerly.

"How do I know? But I got the impression that it might be something pretty personal. Like a photograph or maybe a diploma. Something that wasn't very big."

"But if his father's stealing it was driving Brad crazy, don't you think it must have been something more important than that?"

"Could be. I don't know."

"So," Caro said, "was that what you were looking for in the cellar?"

"Yeah," Deb replied. "That was the only place I could think of. When we were kids playing hide-and-seek, that's where Brad always hid. The rest of us, maybe not Andy, were scared to go look in there."

"But you did anyway," Caro said.

"Yeah. For all the good it did me. All I got was a knock on the head from you."

"Let's face it," Caro said. "I almost got a heart attack from you."

Deb jumped up. "So now we're even, all right? So stop hounding me."

Caro shook her head. "No promises. You might remember something else."

Chapter 15

It was dark on Pier Road. Caro, walking back to Las Mariposas after talking to Deb, kept wishing she had brought a flashlight. The shadows on the road seemed to swallow her up. The trees beside the asphalt met overhead, adding to the feeling. Once her eyes adjusted to the darkness, however, she was able to follow the road slowly.

She guessed that she was halfway back to Las Mariposas when ahead of her she saw a small circle of light bouncing on the asphalt. Fear filled her and she plunged into the trees beside her. And into a thick growth of brambles. She swore under her breath as she jumped back onto the road.

The light swung in her direction and Andy shouted, "Caro! Caro, is that you?"

"What's left of me," she called. "I left half my skin on a vicious plant."

"Sorry I scared you. Are you okay?"

"Probably. I have a few scratches, but I'll live. And am I ever glad you brought a light."

"It helps," Andy said and they started walking up the road. "Well, did you get anything?"

Even though it was too shadowy to see his face, she smiled up at him. Andy rarely asked unnecessary questions. He didn't ask what she had been up to or if she had seen Deb. Just, "Did you get anything?"

"I think so," she answered. "But I'm not sure what." She went on to tell him what Deb had said and how she had had to pry it out of her. By the time she finished, they were at Las Mariposas. They walked around the back of the house.

"Brad had two or three favorite places," Andy said as they sat in the chairs under the elm, "but not the cellar. He liked to be out in the open. He liked to . . . I guess you could call it meditate. As a matter of fact . . ." Andy stopped, cleared his throat and then went on, " . . . I think that's what he was doing when he was killed. That point of land where the car went over was one of his favorite spots. On bright, clear days you could see the goats on Goat Island. And at night the scattering of lights from the long pier seem to float on the water. It's kind of pretty. Maybe he went to Oak Valley to talk with Mr. Steele. Maybe he didn't. In any case, he had some hard thinking to do so he stopped at the point on the way back. That's my guess." Andy frowned and shook his head briskly. "He would no more have used Miss Matilde's car to kill himself . . . How could anyone think that . . ." He let out his breath and shook his head once more. "The way I figure it," he said slowly, carefully, "the way I think it happened was that he was so upset that he didn't set the brake firmly. And that damned wooden barrier wouldn't have held back a bicycle much less a six-cylinder car."

"Oh, Andy, that's terrible. I'm so, so sorry."

"Well, what happened, happened. And dumping on you won't bring him back."

"It's okay. But you said he had other favorite places."

"He did. All outside though. Nowhere to put anything like Deb described. Unless he dug a hole somewhere and, if he did, what chance do we have of finding that?"

"Not much."

They were silent then. Only the soft rustle of a late-homing bird in the branches above them and, in the distance, the muted whine of a siren intruded into the quiet. Finally, Caro said, "Andy? Remember the day that Sara showed me the Guadalupe shrine and you guessed that I'd been there because you said Sara loved showing it off? Didn't you also say that Brad loved that place too? Is it one of his favorite places?"

Andy, as if awakened from a dream, shot up. "Sure! Sure as the nose on my stupid face it is! I'll bet that whatever he hid is there."

"In the shrine itself? But where?"

"Under the roof. There's an empty space there, like a small-scale attic and it's a perfect place to hide things. I'd forgotten all about it. Come on, let's go look."

"Okay, but let me tell Tía Matilde that I'm back."

"She won't expect you yet. I told her I was going to meet you and added that maybe we'd go down to The Creamery for a coke or something."

"In that case, let's go. But don't forget the flashlight."

They walked through the small meadow without needing the flashlight's beam; the pale light of the moon was enough. After they crossed the wooden bridge Caro stopped and whispered, "Use the light, will you? I thought I saw something moving over there through those trees ahead of us. No, don't! I hear something."

They stood as still as statues. And the only sound they heard was the whispering murmur of the water in the creek. Suddenly, the silence was broken by the grinding sound of footsteps as they pushed up the rocky slope from the shrine. Before the footsteps reached the trail there was a loud gasp, a muffled curse, and a thud.

Andy scanned the wooden path with the beam of the flashlight as they ran forward. Caro tugged Andy's arm. "There's someone on the trail," she whispered.

"Hey!" Andy called as he swung the light on a man running down the path past the shrine. The man ran crouched over, his right arm flung across his face. "Hey!" Andy called again and then he stopped dead in his tracks. "Well," he said, "would you believe it? It's the mayor."

"I believe it, all right," Caro said. "He figured it out before we did. And whatever he took belongs to Tía Matilde. He's stealing. Can't we call the police or something?"

"I don't think so," Andy said grimly. "What did he steal? Where was it? Who saw him? We don't have any answers. They'd just laugh at us."

Caro, whose fists were clenched tightly as if ready for a fight, slowly loosened them. "You're making sense and I don't like it. I wish we'd just chased him and knocked him in the head before we recognized him."

"And be hauled in for attacking an officer of the law?" Andy retorted with a grin.

"I know, I know. Do you think we might have scared him away before he took anything?"

"Not for a minute. But let's go look."

Halfway down the slope Caro said, "Whoops!" and grabbed Andy's arm. "I almost lost my footing," she said. "This must be what we heard. You know, where he slipped and fell. He sure loosened a lot of soil."

Andy, who had been playing the light over by the shrine, now focused it at their feet. "Sure did," he said. "Just be . . . hey, what's that by your foot?"

"A little piece of crumpled up paper," she said, bending over to pick it up. "Well, not so crumpled. Mostly dirty and smashed." She held it under the light. "Look, there are specks of blood on it, fresh blood if I know anything."

"So he did beat us to it," Andy said. "That paper must be part of what he took. He must've had it in his hand when he fell. Straighten it out, Chief. Yeah. It looks like a little piece of writing paper."

"It looks like the *bottom corner* of a sheet of writing paper," Caro said. "And there are all of four words on it. '... *still be near them* ...' Andy! It's got to be a corner from the first page of Don Armando's letter! It's the same writing! I'm sure of it! And the mayor's got it! He's going to steal my aunt's inheritance!"

Andy stared at the torn bit of paper in Caro's hand and in a shaken voice said, "No wonder Brad was thrown into a tailspin. What a dirty mess this is. Well, if it's the last thing I do, I'm going to stop that crook. For Miss Matilde's sake, sure, but, even more, for Brad's."

They walked down to the shrine. One side of the shrine's peaked roof had been pried from the side wall and was pushed off center. Caro said, "Did he ruin it?"

"Not permanently," Andy said. "I'll fix it in the morning." He ran the beam of light under the loosened roof. "Nothing more in there."

"But there's something down here," Caro said and picked up a sturdy screwdriver, holding it by the metal end. "Unless he was wearing gloves, and he couldn't have been; he wouldn't have bled on the paper, we've got his fingerprints all over the handle of this."

Andy grinned. "Evidence for when it goes to court?"

Caro shrugged. "Whatever. Anyway, we can threaten him with the fact that we have it. Oh, and that we have his blood on that paper too. DNA and all that."

"Let's try to outfox him before it comes to that," Andy said. He sat on the fallen log where Caro had found him a couple of days before. "Let's look at that paper again."

Caro paused, frowned and then cried, "Andy! He's coming back! I hear him!"

Andy doused the light. Caro held tightly to the screwdriver and paper and stepped into the shrubbery beside the log.

There was the sound of footsteps on the darkened path. "Hey, you guys," Sara called, "turn on your light! Mine just died."

"Sara," Andy said, "what the heck are you doing out here?"

"That's what I want to ask *you*," Sara said as she trod down the slope. "I was on my way back from Miss Matilde's when I saw a couple of lights blinking down the trail and then I heard Andy yelling. What was that all about?" Then, as she saw the shrine, she added, "Oh, no, who did that?"

"Not us," Caro said. "Come sit down and we'll tell you what's been going on."

"I will, but why were you yelling?"

Andy said, "Just sit down and we'll tell you. Only don't ask questions till we're through."

Between the two of them, Andy and Caro told Sara about seeing the mayor and Deb at the fair, about Caro's visit to Deb and what she had learned, and finished with their encounter with the mayor at the shrine.

"But why did you let him go?" Sara demanded. "Why didn't you go after him?"

"Go? Because he's the mayor," Andy said impatiently. "Anyway, he was gone before we got close. It was pure luck that I caught enough of a glimpse to recognize him."

"You know something," Caro said. "I'll bet he doesn't know that. That we recognized him. Because he sure wasn't wearing a suit. He was wearing old cotton pants."

"What any well-dressed thief would wear," Andy said.

"Oh, no," Sara countered. "He should've been all in black. Maybe even a mask. Like cat burglars."

"Yeah," Andy said. "In any case he's got what we were looking for. And where does that leave us?"

"Well, we've got four words from that first page," Caro said with a long, dejected sigh. "Let's see what we can make of them."

Chapter 16

Caro had trouble falling asleep that night. Images from the hectic day flicked in and out of her mind as abruptly as the scattered scenes in a movie trailer.

Finally, she forced herself to think of something else: home. When she did, she drew in her breath sharply; her longing to be there was so great that it almost hurt. She wanted to be in her own bed, to hear the bedspring that squealed each time that she turned on her side. She wanted to be planning what she would do the next day, like maybe help Ernie tinker with the old Mustang in his backyard, the one he claimed functioned with a carburetor. Or, maybe, if it wasn't too hot a day and her mother didn't beat her to using the kitchen, she would try making that chocolate cake recipe she'd cut out from the newspaper. Or . . .

"No, no, no!" Caro mumbled. She pushed her pillow away and immediately pulled it back. If you're going to lie awake thinking, she argued silently, think of what to do next to help Tía Matilde. Sure, it's a mess, but you talked your way into coming up here and you talked your way into holding back Don Armando's letter from Tía. So, instead of lying here wishing that you were home, lie here and figure out what those four words on the scrap of paper the mayor dropped could mean. Come on, Caro, we all agreed that it would be a good idea to sleep on it, so

129

sleep or figure! Caro stretched and frowned and, in the middle of her next thought, fell asleep.

It wasn't until early afternoon that Sara, Andy, and Caro got together to decide on their next step. Andy had called early the following day to say that he had two fares, one a long haul beyond Oak Valley, that would fill the morning hours. Sara, too, was occupied. She had a dentist's appointment that she had conveniently forgotten until María reminded her. So the meeting that they had agreed would happen first thing after breakfast had to wait.

During the morning Caro helped Matilde make a streusel coffeecake for the next day's breakfast, one that would serve their four guests generously. After that, they made up some small fruit baskets for the guest bedrooms. Caro took them upstairs and put out fresh towels in the two rooms that would soon be occupied. Throughout the hours that she spent with Matilde, Caro found herself wanting to shout, "Look what we found! Here's what's been happening! The mayor's a thief!" But she swallowed back the words. She tried to sound normal, chattering away—which was not normal at all—about her family and friends, and, from the looks that Matilde sent her occasionally, she knew she had done a lousy job. Finally, lunch was over and she drove Matilde to Two Sands to keep an appointment at the bank and another with her insurance agent.

Andy and Sara were waiting under the elm tree when Caro returned to Las Mariposas. "Am I glad to see you guys," she called. "Because I've got to tell you something. I give up. I can't stand it anymore! We've got to tell Tía Matilde what's going on."

"All right," Andy said. "Sure, that's fine. But do you think it can wait until we've explored something? Maybe just an hour or so."

"Why not?" she said, "One hour won't make much difference. Especially since Tía Matilde won't be back for a couple of hours. But I want you to know I'm serious. Anyway, what are we going to explore?"

Sara moved forward eagerly in her chair. "Tell her, Andy, tell her."

"See if you agree," Andy said. "While Sara and I waited for you, Chief, we got silly, playing around with the four words from the scrap of paper we found last night. Since they seemed to be the end of a sentence, we tried crazy beginnings. Sara's favorite was, 'I ate all the chocolate candies because that way I could still be near them.' Mine was something about keeping goldfish by my bed. Actually, none of our sentences was all that funny, but they did have one thing in common. An 'I could' or 'you could' or 'we could' came right in front of those four words in any sentence we came up with. So we figured that Don Armando's words had an 'I could' in front of them too. Which means that whatever he left for Miss Matilde, he left where *he could still be near them*."

"Yes!" Caro said. "And the second part of the letter we have says that the first part tells her where he put *them*. And whatever them is or are, he sure wasn't talking about candies or goldfish, was he? But he wanted them near him."

"Yes, yes!" Sara said. "That's what we figured."

"So *them* are probably in the house," Andy added.

"You guys are great," Caro said. "I'll bet they're in his old bedroom. Maybe in a safe or a place in the closet or something in the walls."

Andy shook his head. "Sorry, Chief, that room doesn't exist anymore. Nearly all the walls were torn down upstairs when Miss Matilde turned this place into a B&B. If there'd been anything in that room, she would've found it then."

Sara said, "So what we figured . . ."

"Of course!" Caro interrupted. "Angela's room! That was his studio, and it wasn't remodeled, was it?"

"Not drastically," Andy answered. "Only paint and . . ."

"And the floors," Sara said. "They refinished the floors."

"The room he used for cleanup and storage is now a bathroom," Andy went on, "but that's all. Your closet, the one under the stairs, was always there. He kept junk like boards covered with canvas in there and old frames and even paintings he'd given up on. The only reason I know this is because after he died that room stayed the way it was for a couple of years. And whenever María came to help Miss Matilde, she brought us along and we were allowed to play in the old studio."

"And you always snooped," Sara said.

"And you always told on me, blabbermouth."

"I think you're right," Caro said. "That's just where we should look. Come on."

They all got up and marched into the house. But once they were in Angela's room, they stood, and looked around hesitantly.

"No sense in looking in the new bathroom," Andy said.

"No," Caro said, "nor in the old desk. Not after what Mr. Jiménez told me about it."

Sara said, "And since the floors were redone, they would've found any loose boards where you could hide things."

"So it's the clothes closet," Caro said. "I'll dump my stuff on the bed, but there's another clothes pole behind that where Angela hung all *her* things. I guess we'll have to pull those out too."

Caro took her clothes from the rod and handed them to Sara. The rod in the back of the closet was packed tightly. Caro called, "Leave room on the bed for Angela's things. She's got scads of stuff. Heavy winter things."

As she pulled Angela's things off the clothes pole, Caro thought, this is a lot of work and probably all for nothing, but I hate to give up. I suppose we *should* do this much, anyway, before we tell Tía Matilde. Maybe, once she hears everything, she'll be able to face the mayor with all that we've learned about him and somehow force him to give up the first page of the letter. Stop dreaming, Caro. Tía Matilde doesn't have it in her to confront anybody; she's too gentle, too compliant for that kind of a showdown. I guess it *is* up to us. She shrugged and let out her breath in a long sigh of frustration. Then, with greater determination, she lifted a heavy wool coat off the rod and passed it to Andy.

Once the remaining garments were off the second bar, the light from a wall sconce brightened up the closet's back area. Here the ceiling angled down toward the floor, but there was still room to stand upright.

"Look, you guys," she called, "there are a couple of boxes stacked up here in back. They look interesting. Do you suppose . . . No," she answered herself, "no, this couldn't be it, or them. Anybody could find them here."

By this time both Andy and Sara were in the closet. Sara pulled a flashlight from her pocket and played its beam on the two cartons. "New batteries," she said and pointed to the flashlight. "I just knew we'd be crawling around some dark places."

"Good thinking," Andy said. "The boxes are both marked, 'Angela Hoffman' and they're taped up too. So that settles that. They're private. We can't look in them."

"No way," Caro said. "Even if we thought these boxes were it, which we don't."

"They look heavy," Sara said. "I wonder what's in them."

"Books," Andy replied. "I'd say books." As they left the closet, he paused and said, "Hand me that flash, Sara." He ran the light around the small room, focusing on the back wall. "When I was a kid I used to think this was a huge closet," he said. "Funny how places seem to shrink when you grow up."

Caro, looking over his shoulder, said, "I wonder why Don Armando made his store room so small. There's lots more space under the stairs, isn't there?"

"Chief," Andy said, "you're a genius. Sure there's more room under the stairs. And why do you think Don Armando closed off part of it?"

"Do you think this could be it?" Caro asked, her voice tense.

"It sure fits the four words we found. He certainly was near it, or *them*, in this closet."

Sara threw her arms around Caro. "We found it!" she said. "Can you believe it? We found it!"

Andy grinned. "Take it easy. Let's move the boxes before you celebrate." Sara squeezed into the closet and dropped to her knees by the two cartons. "Hey, don't crowd me, Sara. Just hold the flashlight on this wall."

The boxes were heavy. Andy and Caro tugged and pulled and, with Sara pressed against the side wall and out of the way, they finally dragged them close to the entrance of the closet.

"That barrier looks solid," Andy said. "Like it was put there to stay there. Maybe they had rats or something that they were trying to keep out."

"Oh," Sara said in a deflated voice. "Like the raccoons we had."

Caro, down on her knees looking at the wooden partition, said, "It looks permanent, all right. It's even got little strips of wood, you know, like moldings, at the top and bottom. Why would anybody make a plain old closet wall so fancy?"

"That's easy," Andy said. "It was probably built by Mr. Jiménez. He's more of a cabinetmaker than a carpenter."

Caro said, "I thought we'd be able to loosen a board or two and just peek through, but it's not that simple, I guess."

Andy got down on the floor beside her. "No, not that simple. Besides, I don't think we have the right to start tearing down Miss Matilde's house. Do you?"

"Well," Caro said with an unhappy little sniff, "loosening a board or two wouldn't be like tearing down anything, but I guess this partition is different."

"Hey, Sara, you're suffocating me." Andy twisted his neck to look back at her. "Move back."

"Okay, okay," Sara said impatiently. "I was just trying to see what that was down in the corner by Caro."

"What is it? Where?" Caro asked, pushing away from the wall. "Not a spider, please."

"No," Sara said with a laugh. "Just above the molding. There's a funny little hole . . . no, not a hole, a little hollow place. See?"

"Lend me the flashlight," Caro said and, with her head bent close to the floor, examined the wooden wall. "Here it is," she said and pushed her finger into the indentation Sara had pointed out. She felt it yield to pressure and heard a metallic click behind the wall. She held her breath as she ran her hand along the side of the wooden wall. When it gave way, sliding inwards, she squealed, "Eureka! Excelsior! Whatever! It's moving!"

The center of the wall, affixed top and bottom to the floor and staircase on a metal rod, rotated inward, opening up the remaining area under the staircase. And, with the flashlight's ray brightening the enclosure, it was easy to see what was hidden there.

There was a heavy hush as the three of them stared into the opening. Sara broke the silence.

"It's only Don Armando's old paintings," she moaned. "That's terrible." Oil paintings, the larger ones stacked neatly along the side walls and the smaller ones at the shallow end, filled the extension under the stairs.

Caro slumped back on the floor. "No wonder Tía Matilde and his wife never could find them."

Andy shook his head tersely. "I guess that does it. We tried. It's time to give up."

"At least we found the way to open that wall," Sara offered.

"I know," Caro replied as she crawled out of the closet. "I suppose that's something. But do you mind if I feel like crying?"

Chapter 17

🦋 They had just finished putting the closet back in order, leaving the two heavy cartons near the entry, when the telephone rang. It was Matilde, ready to return.

"I'll go get her," Andy said. "In case the guests show up early."

Andy was prophetic. Mr. and Mrs. Miller, a middle-aged couple, both plump and soft-spoken, arrived within minutes of his leaving. Caro explained to them that her aunt would return in a minute or two and invited them to please sign the register.

Sara appeared from the kitchen, carrying a tray that held two icy glasses of lemonade and a small plate of Angela's best sugar cookies. "This is for you," she said with a quick little smile. "You must be thirsty."

"Do you mind if we take this up to our room?" Mrs. Miller asked.

"Of course not," Caro said. "I'll carry it up for you." When she returned Sara held out a cookie to her.

"We did all right, didn't we?" she asked. "With the guests, I mean."

"Absolutely," Caro replied. "We know the drill."

Sara grinned, her eyes twinkling. "Too bad we're not that good as detectives."

Caro frowned. "Maybe we shouldn't give up yet. There must be another place where we could look. Think, Sara, think."

"I thought you'd given up. Anyway, it's too late. Andy's probably telling Miss Matilde about everything right this minute."

"I suppose," Caro said, turning away. Sara was right. It was up to Matilde now.

Fifteen minutes later, Mrs. Miller, carrying the tray with the empty glasses, found them in the kitchen. "Sorry," she said, "we can't wait for Mrs. Reyes. We're here for a wedding at Vista Mar Ranch and we have to be there today. We'll be at the ranch most of the time, but we'll be back every night. So we'll need a house key, won't we?"

"Sure," Caro said. "I don't know what's holding up my aunt. I'll get one for you."

It was a good half an hour more before Andy and Matilde returned. It was clear that there was something wrong. Andy, as he walked into the kitchen behind Matilde, shook his head urgently and frowned.

Matilde looked drained. She sighed as she turned to Caro. "Did our guests arrive?"

"Yes," Caro answered. "And they're gone again. They said they wouldn't be around much."

"But they really loved the place," Sara said quickly.

"I gave them a house key. I hope that's all right," Caro added.

Matilde nodded. "Of course. I have a lot to tell all of you, but not now. I have to pull up some figures on the computer and then find time to rest my broken foot. Thank heavens our other guests won't be here till after supper." She hobbled to the door where she turned. "Maybe Andy can share with you some of what's going on. We'll talk later."

As Matilde left the room, both Sara and Caro turned to Andy.

"What?" Caro said. "What happened?"

"It's the mayor again," Andy whispered. "Come on outside and we'll talk."

"The mayor?" Caro exclaimed as soon as the back door had closed behind them. "What did he do this time?"

"Probably had her arrested or something," Sara grunted.

"Not exactly," Andy said. They sat down on the back steps and Andy went on. "To begin with, you guys should know that I didn't tell her any of what we've found out or what we've been doing. It wasn't the right time or place."

"You mean we're not going to tell her at all?" Sara asked.

"Not yet," Andy said. "Just listen. We've got a lot of thinking to do."

"Go ahead," Caro said. She heard her own voice come out hoarse and scratchy, as if the words had scraped her throat. She really didn't want to hear any of this. She wanted to sit there and enjoy the warm afternoon sun while staring happily at the cascading white roses on the low rail fence. Her father was right; sometimes she bit off more than she could chew. All right, maybe this *was* one of those times. She cleared her throat. "Go ahead," she said.

Andy threw her a curious glance. "Okay. Well, when I first got to the bank, Miss Matilde was up near the door saying goodbye to Mr. Lund, the bank manager. I waved and she waved back, and she was just about to come out the door when someone inside called them to come back in. Miss Matilde signaled me to park the car. She was laughing when she did that, grabbing a steering wheel in the air and mouthing, 'Park the car.' She was obviously in a good mood, not like afterwards."

"That's not right," Sara said. "She needs to be happy."

Caro nodded. "Absolutely. So what happened?"

"When I got there after parking the van they were sitting in the manager's corner and there was another man with them. I don't know his name, but I recognized him. He's a friend of the mayor's. Actually, I found out that he's his lawyer. And they were looking at some document, I think it was a letter of intent, a proposal from the mayor to buy Las Mariposas for an astronomical amount. Maybe it wouldn't be an astronomical amount for Santa Barbara or Los Angeles, but for Two Sands, with so much of our land contaminated by the old pottery factory, it was almost crazy."

"How much?" Sara asked.

"I can't tell you," Andy said. "Miss Matilde asked me not to tell anyone. It was stated in the mayor's proposal that only she, Mr. Lund, and his lawyer should know. But I saw the figure when Miss Matilde dropped the papers as she was folding them."

Caro said, "He's pulling a fast one."

"Fast, all right," Andy said. "He knows we recognized him last night, so he got busy this morning."

"I think he thinks we know more than we do," Caro said.

"Probably," Andy replied. "I saw part of the proposal and there was something in it that was darned funny. There was a phrase that went something like, ' . . . all attached and unattached (I think 'attached' was the word) properties are to be included in the sale . . .' And then it pointed out the old roll top desk, of so many drawers and

of such and such wood, as one of the 'unattached properties.' Do you suppose it's worth a lot of money?"

"Not according to Mr. Jiménez," Caro said.
"Remember? He told me all about it."

They were silent for a moment and then Caro sat up
stiffly and said, "It's a decoy! The old desk's a decoy! He
doesn't want Tía Matilde to know that there's something
else here that she really wants!"

"Or knows?" Andy suggested.

"No. I think it's something solid, something material,
that he wants. Why else would he have all that 'attached'
and 'unattached' stuff?"

"Well, maybe that 'unattached' stuff is a smoke
screen," Andy said. "Maybe it's the land he wants after
all."

"No, no, Andy," Caro said quickly. "Don Armando
definitely said he'd left her something and that the first
part of the letter told her where it was."

"You're right. I guess my thinking's getting fuzzy.
Okay, so there's something in this house that the mayor
wants and that Miss Matilde knows nothing about."

"And before she finds out, he wants to get the house!"
Sara cried.

Caro turned to Andy. "She wouldn't sell it, would
she?"

"For the amount he's offering, I think she'll be tempted," Andy replied. "And if she signs that proposal thing,
it'll probably be a legal contract."

"We've got to tell her," Caro said. "Right now."

As she spoke, the back door opened behind them and
Matilde said, "Would you all come in now? I have something to tell you."

"So do we," Sara said eagerly.

Matilde nodded and smiled at her, then turned and limped to the small table in the kitchen. They followed her.

"You were going to rest your foot," Caro said.

"I needed to talk to you even more," Matilde replied. "Andy told you about the mayor's proposal?" When they nodded, she went on. "He's . . . he's offering me too much money for the house and that puzzles me. Of course, we all know he's been trying to get me to leave Two Sands for months. I wasn't sure why, but my guess had been that he wanted me to feel so desperate that I'd sell the house for practically nothing just to get away from him. So his offer has me baffled." She sighed. "But that's not exactly what I wanted to tell you.

"What I want you three to know is that he's pushing me to sign right away, by the end of the business day tomorrow. I just can't do it by then." There was an audible sigh of relief from Caro. Matilde glanced at her and said, "Believe me, I'm giving his offer serious thought. Having made a success of Las Mariposas as a B&B means a lot to me. Against all of Papacito's predictions that I didn't have a head for anything but books, I proved that I could do it! In the last couple of weeks, of course, it was your spunk that gave me the courage to keep it from slipping through my fingers."

Matilde grinned. "But it's not courage that's keeping me from signing Jerome's proposal. Papacito tied my hands when it came to selling the house or anything he thought had value, for that matter. I can't do anything without getting advice and agreement from a lawyer in Santa Barbara who, it so happens, is off for the day." She shook her head slowly and added, "Papacito didn't think I could do anything without a man's advice."

"So after you hear from the lawyer in Santa Barbara, will you sell?" Andy asked.

"Yes, I think so. I'm tired of all the aggravation. If Jerome wants . . ."

"Tía, please, you can't!" Caro cried. "We have something to tell you too!"

"It's important," Sara said, "real important."

Matilde glanced from one face to the other, pausing as she looked at Caro. "You're serious, aren't you?"

"We should have told you before," Caro said, "but I persuaded them not to."

"We *all* agreed to wait a day or so," Andy said.

"All right." Matilde rose from her chair. "But first I need a couple of aspirins and then I'll stretch out on my couch to listen to you. Give me a minute or two."

When Matilde was gone Andy said, "We can't tell her about Brad's part in this; it would kill her."

"So we can't mention Deb either," Caro said. "Or what happened at the Guadalupe shrine because that would bring in Brad."

"What *can* you tell her?" Sara asked.

"Good question," Andy said. "Hold on a minute. Let's think."

"I've already thought," Caro said. "We'll tell her the truth: that we're leaving out a lot of details for now that we can fill in later when she's feeling better. She trusts us. I think she'll buy that."

"Maybe," Andy's face creased into a frown.

"Anyway," Caro said, "I think she'd have trouble believing that Deb stayed hidden in the cellar for three hours and that I attacked her when she came out. Or that the mayor broke the Guadalupe shrine and ran off down the Reyes trail when he heard us coming."

Andy laughed. "It does sound phony."

"I wouldn't believe it," Sara said, "not if I hadn't been there last night."

"So what we're doing," Andy said, "is asking her to hold off on selling the house until she finds whatever Don Armando left her."

Caro said, "It's not as if she'll think it's all in our imagination. We do have the letter we found. Let's start with that. I'll go get it."

They sat on the floor by Matilde's couch as she read Don Armando's letter. Caro had told her how she found it and then all three, interrupting one another, told her of their efforts to figure where the first part of the letter might be.

"We didn't ask you, or tell you anything about this," Caro said, "because we didn't want to add another problem to all those you already had. We thought holding off for a day or two wouldn't matter."

"Besides," Sara added, "we decided that if you had the first part of the letter you'd be rich like Don Armando says, and you weren't, you know, rich."

"Bless Papacito," Matilde said. "He always loved to blow up everything. Rich for the rest of my life. Well, that would be nice, but my guess is that all he left hidden were his memoirs aggrandizing himself and his activities here and in Mexico. And, of course, he would think they were worth a million."

Caro's shoulders drooped as she looked at Andy's somber face and at Sara, who looked as if she was about to cry. "I guess you're right, Tía," she said. "Because when we finally figured where Don Armando might have hidden something for you, all we found was an extension to Angela's closet where he had stashed his old paintings."

"You did? Good," Matilde said. "But it wasn't the pot of gold you were looking for, was it? I'm sorry. Papacito, wherever he is, is probably having a good laugh at having fooled not only his wife and me but you three treasure hunters." She pushed up on the couch and, shaking her head in what appeared to be wonder, said, "How did I deserve you three? Thank you for your concern. You are absolute angels. Even you, Andy. Now stop worrying about me. We have a few hours before the next guests come, so go enjoy the afternoon."

They left, marching through the house and out to the chairs under the elm tree. Sara, crestfallen though she was, had stopped to pick up some of Angela's sugar cookies and they sat munching them silently for a while. Finally, Caro spoke.

"Something's wrong here," she said.

Andy nodded. "Yes."

"What?" Sara asked.

"For one thing," Andy said, "I can't believe that the mayor's dumb enough to offer Miss Matilde that money for the house just based on an eccentric old man's letter."

"Right," Caro said. "He knows something we don't know, including Tía Matilde."

"I know, I know," Sara cried. "He knows that whatever the letter is talking about—you know, the *it* or the *them* —is really, really valuable."

"Yes," Andy said. "And Brad knew it too."

"But Tía Matilde doesn't. She doesn't even believe it's possible. So we're right back where we started, finding where Don Armando hid *it* or *them*. And if that lawyer from Santa Barbara calls, we have no time at all to look."

Andy glanced at his watch. "Actually," he said, "I have no time left now. I have a fare to the Vista Mar Ranch that will keep me for a while."

Sara jumped up. "I have to go too. I have to help my mother serve a dinner. But I'll be here to help with break-fast."

"It's just as well," Caro said. "We wouldn't know where to look, anyway."

The feeling that something was wrong and that she needed to do something about it stayed with Caro through supper and the arrival of the next pair of guests. And into the evening.

As soon as it was dark, Matilde asked Caro to forgive her but, after the day she had had, she needed to have a warm shower and get into bed. She asked her to please check the locks and the night lights both upstairs and downstairs.

"Sure," Caro said. "And I'll leave things ready in the parlor for early morning coffee."

It was a glimpse of Don Armando's little unfinished painting in the parlor that suggested to Caro what she should do next. Look between and behind the paintings in the closet to see if, as Tía Matilde had proposed laughing-ly, there were pages of a memoir hidden there.

In a matter of minutes, with a flashlight in hand, Caro had squeezed apart the clothes on the rods in the closet, moved the wooden wall, and crawled cautiously into the area with the paintings. First, she searched through the small paintings at the far end of the extension. Nothing there. But it was interesting to see how carefully they had been stored, with corrugated cardboard between the paintings. Nor was there anything between or behind the large paintings, except for the cardboard separators. She threw a last look at the pictures. Facing her at the far end was a small painting of a crumbling adobe church that stood on a small rise, with a path leading to a village below it. Curiosity led her to glance again. Yes, there was someone in the church's belfry. Shrugging, she edged out of the extended closet.

I'm tired and hot, she thought as she pawed through Angela's winter clothes, and my knees are getting sore. It's all been for nothing, nothing at all. So if Tía Matilde wants to sell her house, let her sell it. There's absolutely no reason why I . . . In the middle of that thought she stopped dead in her tracks.

Caro closed her eyes, reaching back for a memory. And then, with the recovered memory held close, she pushed her way out of the closet and into the bedroom where she rummaged in her clothes drawer until she found an envelope. She stared at the card in the envelope for a long minute, then she swallowed back her hesitation and reached for her cell phone.

Chapter 18

🦋 The next morning when the phone rang right after the guests' breakfast, Caro's heart beat fast until she learned that it was not the lawyer from Santa Barbara. When Caro returned to the kitchen, Sara turned away from the dishes she was washing to ask, "Did something happen? Was that the lawyer?"

"No," Caro said. "It was Tía Matilde's insurance man. Something to do with her car. You know, the one they dragged up. She looked pretty sad, but she said it was all right. Because now she'll be able to buy another car."

"If she sells the house," Sara said with an impish grin, "maybe she'll be able to buy two or three cars."

Caro said, "Probably." And then, with a little quiver in her voice, she added, "Or if she finds what Don Armando left her, maybe it will be four."

"In that case," Sara said, "I can stay another hour. Where should we look?"

Caro shook her head. "We can't. The guests are still around. We'll have to wait till later." She wanted to tell Sara about the phone call she had made, but she had agreed to say nothing until . . . She glanced up at the kitchen clock. Would the morning never end?

Sara said, "Later's all right. Andy'll be around then and we can think together." She placed a glass she was drying on a shelf in a cupboard by the window, closed the cupboard door, and turned. "Andy fixed the Guadalupe shrine last night. I went with him. I took the virgin flowers and prayed for her to help us find whatever Don Armando's left Miss Matilde. And, you know something? I think she will."

"I'll keep my fingers crossed," Caro said.

"Maybe that will help too," Sara said, her eyes twinkling. And then, "Oh, look, there go the Millers. I'm going to help clean up their room."

Andy came at noon. He looked apologetic as he said, "I'm driving Miss Matilde to Oak Valley. Something about insurance on the car. And then she wants to talk to a school friend of hers, a real estate broker, about the offer on the house."

Caro frowned. "Will it take long? Because maybe she should be here. It might be important. There's no way you could've known about this, and I can't tell you about it. But can I call you on your cell if anything happens, and could you bring her back right away?"

"Sure. But what's all this about? What do you think's going to happen?"

"I can't talk about it, Andy. I'm not good at a lot of things, but I'm good at keeping a promise. And I made a promise after you guys left last night."

"After we left last night?" Andy said slowly. "What could . . ." He stopped himself. "Okay, Chief, I won't hassle you. You'll tell me when you can."

Matilde and Andy were in his car ready to leave for Oak Valley when Caro had a thought that prompted her to run out to them. "Tía," she called, "I forgot to ask. After I finish the upstairs bedrooms, if I have time, is it all right if I pull out some of Don Armando's paintings to look at them?"

Matilde threw her a quick little smile, then nodded. "Why not? I'd like to look at them too. Some of them were pretty good. Would you leave them out till I return?"

"Sure. They won't be in the way."

Caro watched them leave, but, instead of going in, stayed on the porch for a few minutes, scanning Pier Road for a car. Then, with an impatient shake of her head, she turned and went upstairs to finish cleaning the guest rooms. She had just picked up a small pile of used towels on the hall floor and started down the staircase when the doorbell rang. This is it, she thought, trying to hold back the excitement that threatened to leave her breathless. She came. She's here!

At the bottom of the stairs she became aware of the damp bundle in her arms and made a small detour into Matilde's room to drop it on the floor. It was the clear view through Matilde's front windows that showed her a sleek gray Lexus parked in the driveway. Caro's shoulders sagged as she slid the towels behind the door.

The doorbell rang again. To Caro it seemed to have a new sound, urgent, and threatening. All right, Mr. Mayor, she mumbled to herself, I'm coming. "Just a minute," she called. She raced to the rear door, locked it, and raced back up the hall to the front door. There she slid the chain lock in place and opened the door only the two inches the chain allowed.

The mayor, wearing a short-sleeved dress shirt, a loosely knotted tie, and lightweight summer pants, did not look cool. He was red-faced as he said, "Well, young woman, what's the delay? I'm here to see Ms. Reyes. Kindly open the door and tell her I'm here."

Caro swallowed hard. "If you'll give me your name, I'll tell her you were here. She's not at home right now."

The mayor's face grew redder. "Well, where is she?" he demanded.

"I think she's in Oak Valley. On some kind of business."

"I'll just come in and wait for her. You go on about your work."

Caro shook her head. "I'm sorry. I can't let you in. Tía Matilde said I wasn't to let anyone in." Caro clenched the edge of the door so tightly that her knuckles turned white. What if the car she was looking for came right now? What would she do? She stared at the mayor's well-polished shoes as if they held the answer.

"That's nonsense," the mayor said. "Do you know who I am? Just open the . . ."

"I just remembered," Caro said quickly. "She's going to see a man about her car insurance in Oak Valley. I think his name is Naylor. If you're in a hurry to see her, maybe you could catch her there."

The mayor glanced at his watch. "Well, now you're making sense. I'll catch her at Naylor's."

Caro felt limp as she watched him walk to the Lexus. She stayed at the door as he slid into the front seat of the car, made a phone call and backed out of the driveway in a burst of speed that made his tires squeal.

In the kitchen, drinking a tall glass of water and looking out the window at the pleasant back garden, Caro began to unwind. Still, when someone knocked on the back door, she stiffened. But the knock was followed quickly by María's voice calling, "Matilde? Matilde, ¿qué pasa? Are you all right?"

"I'm sorry," Caro said as she opened the door. "I had to lock it. Tía Matilde went with Andy. Remember?"

"Sí, sí," María said. "It's just that we never lock the back door. But if you're alone, está bien. Lock it. I'm going up the stairs to clean the bathrooms and do the vacuum."

"I already made the beds and vacuumed," Caro told her. "I don't think I did a good job with the bathrooms, though."

"You and Sara have done enough for one day. I have heard all about the breakfast. Sara's gone with her father to buy some new shoes. No, no, not for her, for her father. He needs someone to push him into the store, or else . . ." María shrugged. "You should rest now. Matilde will need you when she returns. Go. Rest."

"All right," Caro said, "but not quite yet."

The kitchen clock said one o'clock as she went into her bedroom. It was one thirty by the time she had brought out three large paintings from the closet's extension. She moved them with great care, keeping the corrugated cardboard separators on them as protection. She leaned them against the bed and then brought out four small pictures. These she placed against the big desk and on two chairs.

María, on one of her trips to the kitchen, looked in on her. "Ah," she said. "Sara told me you had found them. They're pretty, no?"

Caro nodded. She stood back and, one by one, looked at the paintings. Yes, they are pretty, she thought, but there's a sad feeling about them, a desolate feeling, as if the painter was all alone in the world. Well, maybe he was. And maybe he asked for it. My mother tried to be friends with him, but, finally, even *she* had to give up.

The doorbell rang, interrupting her thoughts. She took a deep breath, counted to ten to slow down her racing heart and hurried to the door. She opened it only the two inches that the chain lock permitted. "You're here," she said, "thank you," and threw the door wide open.

"With a friend and colleague," the woman on the porch said, indicating the man standing beside her. He was a slim man, trim and tall, with sharp eyes and an alert manner. He smiled and nodded as the woman said, "This is Karl Woods from Santa Barbara. May we come in?"

"Yes, of course," Caro said. She led them into the parlor. She was about to say more when the woman spoke.

"Here, Karl," she said as she stood by the small picture on the east wall. "It was because I had seen this painting that I was persuaded to make this hurried trip. When Will and I were here a couple of weeks ago, Mrs. Reyes told me that it was an unfinished painting by her grandfather." She turned to Caro. "She called it a pa . . . a . . . ."

"A 'Papacito', Mrs. Brown," Caro said with a smile. "That means 'little father.' That's what she called her grandfather, my great grandfather."

Karl Woods nodded, turned back to the framed picture on the wall, and continued to examine it closely.

Mrs. Brown said, "And you say you found several other paintings by this man in your closet? What did your aunt have to say about that? Was she surprised?"

"A little," Caro replied. "But she has another big problem on her mind right now , so she kind of ignored them."

"*Ignored them?* That's hard to believe," Mrs. Brown said. "May we talk to her, please?"

Caro bit her lip. "She's not here." The man at the painting looked up and shot a quick look at Mrs. Brown. She shrugged in a gesture of bewilderment. "Please," Caro hurried on to say, "remember I told you last night that someone wants to buy the house for a lot of money, almost too much, if my aunt signs the paper today? Well, that's why she had to go talk to someone about it right away. And the reason I begged you to come today is that I was afraid the paintings would go with the house if she sold it, and what I heard you say a couple of weeks ago was that paintings done by a man called Varo were worth a lot of money . . ."

"A great deal of money, miss," Karl Woods said from the east corner of the room. "Probably more than this house is worth. If this little painting here were to prove to be an unfinished Varo, it alone would be worth a considerable sum."

"I know," Caro said eagerly. "I don't mean I *really* know, what I mean is that the other pictures say 'Varo' on them, some with dates and . . ." She turned to Mrs. Brown. ". . . and you said that Varo paintings nearly always had a person in them, kind of hidden away somewhere, didn't you?"

"I did. And you remembered. You're an alert young woman. Now, where are these paintings? I've got to see them."

"Sure," Caro said, "but please let me explain something first. My aunt's had a lot of problems lately so I didn't tell her you were coming because I didn't want her worrying about what I'd done, you know, having the nerve to call you, and then maybe having her be disappointed too. I'm really sorry she's not here. But I can call her as soon as we look at them."

"I'm afraid that won't do," Karl Woods said. "You're sixteen, maybe seventeen, aren't you, miss?" When Caro nodded, he added, "We have no adult authorization to look at these paintings and, if they are Varos — good God, if they are — we have no acceptable witnesses to say we didn't cart off one or two. No, Susan, it won't do."

Susan Brown sighed. "You're right, of course. Call your aunt now, dear."

"Sure." Caro returned from the telephone discouraged. "There's something wrong with Andy's cell phone," she said. "I can't make a connection." She looked from one to the other of the couple in the parlor pleadingly. "Are you sure you . . ." She stopped as she caught sight of María coming down the staircase. "But there's María," she said brightly. "And she's the adult in charge here. María," she called, "please come in."

María walked into the parlor, a shy smile of welcome on her face.

"Mrs. Brown, Mr. Woods," Caro said, "this is Mrs. Ruiz. She works here. She's an old friend of my aunt's and she also knew my great grandfather. She'll give you permission to see the pictures and she'll stay with us the entire time."

Caro nodded vigorously at María who looked at her curiously for a moment and then smiled and said, "*¿Cómo no?*"

Mr. Woods grinned at Susan Brown. "I guess that will do, don't you?"

Mrs. Brown nodded and, with Caro leading the way, the four of them went down the hall to see the paintings.

Mr. Woods and Mrs. Brown said very little to Caro or María as they examined the framed paintings. "Canvas on stretcher board," he muttered to Mrs. Brown at one point. "See there," Mrs. Brown said, pointing to an almost indistinguishable figure in a rowboat at another time. And then, apparently, they were done because they turned to face Caro and María, who were sitting by the television set.

"These," Mr. Woods said to Caro, "could, should and, in my opinion, *must* be Varos, but they will need expert confirmation to finalize their authenticity. As for provenance . . ." He turned to María. "You knew the man who painted these?"

"*Sí*. Oh, yes," María said. "I knew him for many years. I was very young when he came here, and he was already very old."

Mrs. Brown, seated on the end of the bed, said, "Tell us about him, please. What was he like?"

María glanced at Caro, then said, "He was a strange man but very close to his family. He spent most of his time in his studio or up in the hills painting."

"And you saw him painting?" Mr. Woods asked.

"*Pues no*. Not in his studio. But in the hills and by the creek, yes, many times. He did more than paint. *Bueno*, he had the walnut groves and he saw that they grew well and that the workers did what they were there to do. He was not a trusting man, you see. One night he brought to my husband and me a metal box that held personal papers and he asked us to keep it for him. But not before he showed us that the box had nothing but his papers. You see? He did not trust us too much. As things happen, the box was broken into. Burglars got into our house. Whoever they were, when they opened it up and found nothing but papers, they left them all scattered on the floor." María shrugged. "*Pues*, who would want letters and wedding pictures, a baptismal certificate, and ancient passports?"

"So you saw his baptismal certificate," Mr. Woods said quickly. "What did it show?"

"*Pues, nada*. Nothing more than the priest's signature and Don Armando's name."

"Which was?" Mr. Woods asked softly.

"Don Armando's full name," María said. "Víctor Armando Reyes Olmeda. Why did you want to know?"

One-hour-and-a-half later, Susan Brown, Karl Woods, Matilde and María were seated in the parlor while in the kitchen Andy and Caro made coffee and searched for cookies.

"So we *had* found Miss Matilde's inheritance in the closet," Andy was saying, "and we figured it was just an old man's stuff. Can you believe us?" He shook his head. "Talk about a bunch of ignoramuses. So, according to Mr. Woods, Miss Matilde will probably be a rich woman."

Caro grinned as she looked up from where she was rummaging in the freezer. "Anyway, we found out in time."

"*You* found out in time," Andy said. "Lucky for everyone you have a good memory."

"Lucky for everyone," Caro replied, "that the Browns were guests two weeks ago. And lucky, too, that we served early coffee in the parlor and not in the kitchen the way we had planned. Otherwise, Mrs. Brown wouldn't have seen that little picture and I wouldn't have overheard what she said about it."

"I still say that your good memory was the critical factor."

"No way, Andy. Things had to happen just the way they did. Like with the mayor. After he found the first page of Don Armando's letter, he probably sneaked in the house and looked at the paintings. And then talked to someone about their value. What a rotten creep! All that 'attached' and 'unattached' stuff in the agreement he wanted Tía Matilde to sign." Caro shuddered. "Would she really have sold the house?"

"Let's not even go there," Andy said. "It scares me." He placed a filled coffee cup on a tray beside three others, turned and said, "Did you find any cookies?"

"Yes. And they're chocolate chip."

They carried the tray and cookies into the parlor. When María jumped up to help them, Matilde said, "Please sit down, María. Mr. Woods has a question to ask you."

Karl Woods said, "I suppose it's you, Ms. Reyes, that I should ask. May I see the baptismal certificate that María told us about earlier?"

Matilde looked blank. She tilted her head and said, "María?"

"Don Armando's papers," María said. "The ones in the box that Juan brought you when Don Armando died."

Matilde said, "But I haven't seen them. I wondered why Papacito had no personal papers." She paused and glanced nervously at María. "Do you suppose . . ."

"¡Sí! ¡Sí!" María burst out. "¡Ese hombre! He didn't even bring them to you. For sure they're still high in the corner of the closet where we hid them. I'll bring them." She scooted out of the parlor and down the hall toward the kitchen.

Matilde smiled and said, "It's all right, Mr. Woods. The papers will be there. In all the turmoil of my grandfather's death, María simply forgot to prompt her husband enough times. As hardworking as Juan is, he needs a little shove now and then to awaken his memory."

"Don't we all," Mrs. Brown said just as the doorbell rang.

Caro glanced at Matilde and, at a nod from her, went to answer the door. She threw it open.

"Well, where is she?" the mayor said loudly. "She had already left Naylor's place when I got there, so I drove up to Elena's ranch. And all for nothing. Matilde, it seems, had changed her mind about going there." He glanced beyond Caro's shoulders to where Andy stood. "Andy! Where did you take her? I need to find her. Where is she?"

"I'm right here, Jerome," Matilde said quietly from behind Caro. Cane in hand, she hobbled up to the door. "Go talk to Mrs. Brown, Caro," she whispered and then turned to the mayor. "I have some business associates in the living room, so I can't ask you in. But I'll come out to the porch where we can talk."

"All right," the mayor said peevishly. "Maybe it's just as well they're here. I suppose they're adults. Your business associates, I mean. They can witness your signature on the contract we gave you at the bank yesterday."

"Contract?" Matilde asked.

"Don't be so fussy, Matilde. The letter of agreement about selling the house."

"Oh, that?" Matilde said. "I'm sorry, Jerome. I gave it a lot of thought. But I didn't want to be tempted by your generous offer any longer, so I tore it up an hour ago."

"No, Matilde, you can't do that," the mayor said hurriedly. "But it does not matter, I have another copy in my briefcase."

"Jerome, I'm not interested," Matilde said firmly. "And I don't have time to talk anymore. I'm busy discussing the disposal of Don Armando's paintings. As you know, he left me quite a collection."

Caro, still standing at the front door, turned and grinned at Andy. "Look at the mayor," she said, "just look at him! I think he's going to melt like the Wicked Witch of the West."

Chapter 19

Deb. Caro knew that it was time to tell Deb. Now that an excited Sara had been brought up to date, now that the paintings had been numbered and listed and returned to their hiding place, and now that, finally, everyone was gone, Caro knew that no matter how tired she was, she had to walk down Pier Road to the house with the blue shutters and tell Deb what had happened. Deb deserved to know that Brad's efforts had helped to save the Varo paintings from his father's trickery. Maybe in some small way knowing that would lessen Deb's pain, if not her sadness.

Caro went down Pier Road slowly while images from the afternoon's events whirled through her mind. Matilde's face losing all color, her eyes wide in disbelief when she learned of the paintings' value. The arrival in the middle of the afternoon of Don Armando's lawyer, Alejandro Paz from Santa Barbara, a gray-haired man in his sixties who was as soft-spoken as he was capable, and who took over for Matilde almost immediately. The hubbub of phone calls and voices making arrangements for the authentication and temporary protection of the paintings, including the hiring of a guard that both Karl Woods and Alejandro Paz could agree on. The ecstatic look on Sara's face as, with her thick braid swinging across her back and a bouquet of white roses dangling from her hand, she rushed across the little meadow to thank the

Virgen de Guadalupe. And, of course, the image that was the clearest and most satisfying to Caro: the mayor and his remarks as he had walked off the porch early in the afternoon. "You never had a head on your shoulders, Matilde," he shouted from the bottom of the steps. "You find a few old paintings hidden under a staircase and you decide they're worth a king's ransom. You'll regret it. My offer to buy the house is off. Completely off. Goodbye." Caro, remembering, grinned. In his anger, the mayor had given himself away. Nobody had told him where the paintings had been found, but he had known.

As she trudged down Pier Road, Caro was so deep in her thoughts that she failed to see the red convertible coming up the road until its brakes shrieked and it came to a skidding halt beside her.

"Hey!" Deb called. "What's with crazy Mayor Poole? He's been up and down this road at least a dozen times today."

"I know. I was just coming to see you. Let's go back up to the house and I'll tell you."

Deb hesitated. "I've got things to do," she said, "but, okay, get in. We'll talk for a minute."

At Las Mariposas they went into the back garden, where Caro dropped into a reclining chair. "I'm beat," she groaned, "big time." Then she went on to tell Deb all that had happened since she had left her a couple of nights before. Deb seemed to show little interest as she listened. But when she heard how Matilde had squelched the mayor she grinned and nodded. Caro grinned back. "We never could have found the paintings without you," she finished.

"Without Brad," Deb said.

"Without Brad and you," Caro added. "But I guess it was Brad. He kept getting in his father's way, slowing him down."

"Yeah," Deb said, "in time for you to get here and start nosing around. Guess it was a good thing you did that. You were a pain in the neck though." She was quiet for a moment, looking up through the tree branches, then she said, "It would be nice to think that Brad knows how it all worked out."

"Sara says he knows."

Deb bent over in her chair and dug out a weed in the grass by her foot. Finally, she looked up and said, "She does?"

"Sure. But, just in case, she's down at the virgin's shrine making sure that someone passes the word to him."

"That's good," Deb said with a quick little smile. She stood up. "How long are you going to be around? Here. At Las Mariposas I mean."

"Till the end of next week," Caro replied. "Angela will be back by then, and I've got things to do before school starts, so . . ."

"So then let's say goodbye now," Deb said. "I'm off to Paris tomorrow to meet my mother and we'll be there for a while."

"Paris, wow. That's great."

Deb shrugged. "She's been all over Europe in the last few weeks. I could've gone with her but . . ."

"But you wanted to be with Brad, I'll bet," Caro said quietly.

Deb nodded. She bit her lip and said, "See you sometime then. Goodbye." With that she turned abruptly and marched around the corner of the house.

Andy awakened her.

"Oh, my gosh," Caro said, glancing around the shadowy back garden, "it's dark already. I must've fallen asleep after Deb left."

"You did. Miss Matilde and I have been watching you."

"While I snored, probably."

"I didn't say, 'hearing you.' I said, 'watching you.' Besides, we didn't have time to listen; we've been busy. The man to guard the paintings arrived, and we've been moving you to the Ocean Room."

Caro stiffened. "*You* have?"

Andy grinned. "Actually, María has. I just carried up your duffel bag and shoes."

"You mean everybody's here?"

"Everybody. We warned them about Sleeping Beauty and they all tiptoed by you." Andy bent over her. "But I get to wake you up."

Caro lifted her face to his. "So you're Prince Charming," she said. "What kept you? I'm tired of sleeping."

Back in the house Caro found a party in the making in the kitchen and a stocky, amiable, and tough-looking man standing by Angela's and her bedroom door.

"Sorry to move you out, miss," he said, "but I guess you know why."

"Sure," Caro answered. "No problem at all. You haven't seen the Ocean Room."

In the kitchen Matilde was at the counter, lifting a large chocolate cake out of a bakery box. There was yellow writing on the cake's top. "Hey, it's for Angela," Caro said.

"She's back? I feel like Rip Van Winkle. How long did I sleep?"

"Not that long," Matilde said. "Read it again."

"It says, 'Thank you, *angels*,'" Sara said. "Not 'Angela.' Miss Matilde's giving *us* a party."

"A little one," Matilde added, "out under the elm."

María, who was fixing a salad in a large wooden bowl, dried her hands on a towel and opened the back door. "*Por fin*," she said. "Juan is here with our food."

"Pizzas," Sara said delightedly. "And we remembered that you liked anchovies."

Andy shut the refrigerator door. "I've got the drinks and the paper plates," he said. "And I'm starving."

For some reason that she could not explain, Caro closed her eyes and tried to imagine herself at home in her own kitchen encircled by the members of her family, Mamá, Papá, Luisa, and Joey. But the image would not hold. She opened her eyes. This was the place that, for this moment, captured her mind and filled her with warmth: Sara, carrying the chocolate cake outside; María, with the huge wooden salad bowl; Andy, juggling cans of soda and paper plates; and Tía Matilde, scanning the kitchen as she searched for her cane.

Caro grabbed the cane from where it leaned against the small table and handed it to Matilde. "Here, Tía," she said. "I'll help you down the back steps."

In a little more than half an hour the pizzas were gone and half of the chocolate cake. And, suddenly, everyone was quiet. The quiet lasted for a few long moments, long enough for two or three crickets to start a tentative chirping. The chirping stopped when María stood up.

"Juan and I will take these things to the kitchen," she said. "Eh, Juan?"

Mr. Ruiz, catching a glance from his wife, stood up and said, "Then off to bed for me. Saturday is a long hard day." Andy helped with the cleanup.

When he returned, Matilde said, "I wanted a moment to thank you three for what you did for me."

"Not just us," Caro said. "Brad too."

Matilde nodded. "Yes, I know. Andy has told me a bit about that."

"One thing led to the other," Andy said. "But it was the Chief's—I mean Caro's—squeezing bits of information out of Deb and then remembering what Mrs. Brown had said that brought it all together."

Sara said, "Miss Matilde, would you really have sold the house?"

"I think so. I was very tired of fighting Jerome. Even though Alejandro Paz says Jerome's ownership of the paintings probably wouldn't have held up in court, Jerome would have ended up with them, or some of them, anyway, because I couldn't see spending my life fighting legal battles with him." She smiled at them. "That's what Jerome was counting on. He knows how easily I give in. That's why the last few weeks made him panic. He thought I would have given up before this, but he didn't realize that you three were bolstering up my courage . . . And waging an underground campaign too."

Sara asked, "But are Don Armando's paintings really worth a whole lot of money? I know they're pretty and all that, but . . ."

"Yes, Sara," Matilde answered. "I think I can safely say that they're worth a great lot of money. While we were waiting for the pizzas and for Caro to wake up, I got a phone call from Karl Woods. After much legal haggling earlier today, Alejandro Paz allowed Mr. Woods to take two paintings with him. In Santa Barbara, Mr. Woods showed them to another art expert who is ready to swear that they are genuine Varos."

"So that means that you'll be rich," Sara said. "Miss Matilde, isn't that cool?"

"It's cool, all right, Sara. Because I can share it with others. I won't know how much for a while, but I wanted you three to know that. And because it's something he has to know right now, I have to say this to Andy. Choose any of the universities that have accepted you, Andy. Don't worry about the cost anymore. I know it's a little late, but, hurry, go home right now and write the appropriate letter, fill out the forms and don't argue with me. Do it."

Caro turned to Andy. "My aunt's a tough woman, Andy. Didn't you know? Better do what she says."

Chapter 20

🦋 It was Friday again. One week had gone by since Karl Woods and Susan Brown had made their special trip to Las Mariposas. In that week there had been a lot of endings, a lot of beginnings, and a lot of arrivals of B&B guests.

On Tuesday Caro moved back down to Angela's bedroom. That was the day when the paintings, under Mr. Woods' careful supervision, were removed to a high-security storage unit near his gallery. On Wednesday the late summer guests filled Las Mariposas and kept everyone, from Matilde to a newly recruited young Tony, busy cleaning, shopping, and preparing breakfasts. Except for several telephone calls about the progress of the authentication and about the legalities of how the paintings would be handled, the thinking and planning that went on at Las Mariposas was all about the B&B guests.

On Thursday, while Sara and she were making up the guests' beds and dusting, it dawned on Caro that this was to be her last full day here and a heavy sadness filled her. Sara, with her usual optimism, said, "We won't let you miss us. I'll come down and see you. And Andy, you know, is going to pick that college near Los Angeles."

That's nice, Sara, she had wanted to say, but it will never be the same. Something special happened to me here. Papá kept saying that I wasn't ready to shoulder responsibility, but in these last few weeks I learned that I

167

could. And I'm always going to thank Tía Matilde for that. She let me help her and that let me find my strengths. But, glancing at Sara across the bed they had just finished making up, she said none of this. Instead she had said, "I'll be seeing you for sure. I'm not going to lose touch with any of you."

Thursday night Matilde and Caro had supper at the small table in the kitchen. When they were through, Matilde said, "There'll be a good deal of money from the paintings for your mother. After all, Papacito was her grandfather too. But I'm going to put aside some money just for you. No, no, don't argue." Matilde took a sip of coffee and smiled. "You've learned to make good coffee, Caro. I'm going to miss it." She put the cup down. "Now about that car you were earning money for. Is it safe? Do you need a newer one?"

"No, no, Tía," she had said. "It's safe. Ernie's fixing it up and he's a great mechanic. My mother says Ernie can't wait for me to see it."

After supper Andy and she said their goodbyes. "I can't cancel tomorrow's fare," Andy said, "and I'll be gone up in Oak Valley all morning. Come on, let's go where we can talk. But first, a root beer float at The Creamery for Brad. I wish you had known him." Back at Las Mariposas he had kissed her quickly and said, "I'll call you tomorrow. Maybe twice."

Now it was Friday morning. The hassle of breakfast was over. The guests were gone for the day. And, because both Sara and María had helped, the guests' rooms were all done, and it was only ten thirty.

Caro put her toothbrush and comb into her duffel bag and zipped it up. In two hours, maybe less, her mother and father would arrive. They would arrive in time for a quick lunch and then Caro would go home with them. She stood by the open hall door and let her gaze circle Angela's room: the old desk, the TV corner, the closet with its hidden riches. Then, with a quick look at her watch, she turned away. She just had time for a walk down the Old Creek road.

The grass in the little meadow was drier now, she thought, as she crossed it. The creek, too, was changed; it was a thinner stream than it had been when she first came. Only the virgin's shrine was the same. There was the usual small glass with fresh flowers. Pink geraniums this time. She sat for a moment on the log near the shrine and listened to the indignant chirping of a bird on a branch above her. In a moment she rose and continued down the trail.

When she reached the Old Creek bridge on Hill Street she waved to Mr. Jiménez. He sat on a bench on the porch of his neat gray house.

"*Buenos días,* señorita," he called. "Won't you sit for a minute?"

"Thank you, but no, Mr. Jiménez." When she was at the foot of the porch steps she added, "I want to walk out to the pier and I don't have much time. I'm going home in a couple hours."

"Ah. Well, then, I'm glad for the chance to say good-bye. You have been a busy girl, eh? Looking for and finding a treasure, no? I have heard a word or two."

"I guess everyone will hear soon. Goodbye. It was nice knowing you." Caro swung around to go and then, abruptly, turned back. "I have a question. I hope you can answer it." She sat on the top of the porch steps and said, "I know Don Armando was afraid to sell his paintings,

afraid that he'd be found, but do you know why? Do you
know what he was afraid of?"

"All I know, young lady, is what my mother told me.
And what she knew she knew because when Don
Armando first arrived he hired my father as a body-
guard."

"A bodyguard? Wow. He was scared."

"He had a right to be scared, I think. It seems that in
the town where he lived in Mexico he was involved in
something—my parents never knew what it was—but it
caused the death of a rival's son. The grieving father
turned right around and hired assassins to murder Don
Armando's daughter and her husband, leaving their two
little girls orphans."

"No! How awful!"

Mr. Jiménez nodded. "That's when Don Armando fled
Mexico with his wife and the two little girls. He came to
the United States. He avoided the large cities and the
towns where artists congregated. For him Two Sands was
the perfect place to hide. It was more or less a dying little
town. The pottery plant was closed, leaving the land on
the east side of the hills somewhat poisoned. You know
about the walnut groves. So he spent the rest of his life
hidden here, a fearful old man."

Caro sighed. "Poor Papacito. Even if it was all his
fault."

"No one knows about fault. That it was a tragedy is all
we know for sure."

Caro got up. "Thank you. It makes me understand Tía
Matilde a little better." She paused and then said, "I wonder where my mother got her gutsiness?"

"And you, señorita?" Mr. Jiménez said with a smile.

"Oh, my mother for sure. How else would I have learned to stamp my foot?"

Caro walked down Pier Street past the busy shops, across the ocean highway, and on to the wooden pier. There, with the rising seabreeze blowing softly through her hair, she stayed deep in her thoughts, knowing that what she had just heard would take a while to absorb. In a few moments she turned her back to the sea and, with a long look at the buildings along the ocean highway and those lodged against the hills, she said a silent goodbye to Two Sands.

As she walked up the Old Creek road she wondered if her mother knew what she had just learned. Probably not. Nor Tía Matilde. Maybe it was just as well. What Mr. Jiménez had just told her would remain her secret. She was trudging by the virgin's shrine when she heard her name called.

"Caro! I've been waiting for you. Miss Matilde said you'd be coming by here."

"Andy!" She raced down the pathway to the shrine, almost sliding into his arms. "You came back."

"I had to say a real goodbye."

"I'm glad," she said and took his hand as they walked toward the meadow. "Wait till you hear what I have to tell you."

Also by Ofelia Dumas Lachtman

Call Me Consuelo

A Good Place for Maggie

The Girl from Playa Blanca

Leticia's Secret

Looking for La Única

The Summer of El Pintor

The Trouble with Tessa